HUMAN-SHAPED FIENDS

CHANDLER MORRISON

DEATH'S HEAD PRESS

an imprint of Dead Sky Publishing, LLC
Miami Beach, Florida
www.deadskypublishing.com

ISBN: 9781639510160

Cover Art: Justin T. Coons

The "Splatter Western" logo designed
by K. Trap Jones

Book Layout: Lori Michelle
www.TheAuthorsAlley.com

Author Photo: Mark Maryanovich

For Marissa D.

"The future always looks good in the golden land, because no one remembers the past."

—Joan Didion

PROLOGUE

THE DEVIL WINDS sweep along the corpse-strewn streets and swirl the fires into strange, dancing shapes as Los Angeles burns. Columns of smoke rise from flaming buildings, curling up into the black night sky where no stars can be seen. Men and women and children, wounded and bleeding and dying, cry out for their deaf God and absentee saviors and mothers long or newly dead. Horses with splayed-open stomachs and vacant black eyes lie sprawled and tangled in the dirt and the dust as huge green flies circle their spilt blood and cooling entrails. A figure charred well beyond recognition hangs swaying from a streetlamp. Tiny fires still crackle along the folds of its soiled clothes.

Sheriff James Barton stands at the window of the county jailhouse and looks out at the carnage on the street through the soot-smudged glass, smoking a cigarette and worrying a plug of cocaine chewing gum between his molars. His face is drawn, its faint stress lines caked with dirt and ash. His clothes are torn and bloody. There are dark bruises on his neck. His badge is gone.

"Not long now," he says, watching a new crowd of

rioters advance from the south. They're still a few hundred yards away, a black and indistinct mass moving and shifting in the night beneath the bobbing yellow tips of their torches. "They'll be here soon. They're comin' for you." He spits. "I've not decided yet if I'm gonna hand you over to 'em or not."

"They want you, too, cerdo. You know it. You know they want your blood as well as mine." The voice is clear, composed. Confident.

Barton nods slowly, dragging deeply from his cigarette. "Yeah. I know it. But I reckon they want yours a whole lot more. If they'll settle for one or the other, if it comes down to you or me—well, like I said, I've not decided just yet."

"This is about a lot more than me. I'm just one asesino out of many. You stand for something mucho bigger than that."

Barton pushes his hat back with the tip of his thumb and turns around. He crushes out his cigarette in a clay ashtray on his desk and then walks very slowly over to the holding cells, the heels of his boots kicking dust up off the floor. He stands before the bars and peers into the shadows where the silhouette of the boy sits on the cot, still and calm as a monk. "You don't know anythin' about that," Barton says quietly. "You got no idea what I stand for or what I don't."

"I know your city is en fuego, cerdo. I know many people you are supposed to protect are now dead. Blood and fire, cerdo. Whatever you thought you stood for once, that is what you stand for now—blood and fire."

Barton looks over his shoulder. The crowd is nearing. The fevered sounds of their shouts have risen above the nearby cries of the wounded, drowning them out in a clamorous din. He looks back at the boy. "There's somethin' I have to know," he says. "Before they get here, before I decide what I'm gonna do with you—there's somethin' you're gonna have to tell me. Somethin' I just gotta know."

CHAPTER 1

SEVERAL WEEKS EARLIER, on a hot September evening in the San Gabriel Valley when the sun was low in the red sky and the palm trees rose like great impaled spiders in the darkening dusk, the murder of a man named Jim Ellington set off a violent chain of events that would bring Los Angeles to its knees.

"Go'n and round up the last of these here cattle," Ellington said to his son, Grady, who was staring at something in the distance. "Quit dreamin' about supper and we might just get back home to your mother in time for the real thing to still be hot, hear?"

"Someone's comin', Pa," said Grady, pointing toward the hills. "You reckon maybe it's Indians?"

Ellington grunted and took out his smudged and battered spyglass, extending it and lifting it to his eye, aiming it in the direction of his son's finger. He looked for a long while before lowering it and grunting again. He gazed around at the lazily roaming cattle and at his nearby horse, which was distractedly chewing grass and staring westward at the sinking sun. The land was still and quiet and there was no wind. Ellington spat and said to Grady, "I don't hardly know what they is. Probably nothin', but I don't rightly like the looks of 'em. Go'n over yonder and hide in them there rocks. They ain't seen us yet and there ain't no use in 'em knowin' there's two of us."

"But Pa, if they's lookin' for trouble—"

"Do as I say, boy."

"I'm near enough a grown man, Pa. I don't—"

"Boy," said Ellington, his voice becoming tinged with sharp urgency and diminishing patience, "don't make me tell you again. Now, if things go bad, you just stay hid till the dust settles. If somethin' happens to me, you wait and then you just take the horse and ride back home as fast as her legs'll carry ye. Now *go*."

Grady bit his lip and gave one last glance toward the faraway shapes before doing as he'd been told.

Ellington was packing his things into his saddlebags when the figures came into full view. He left his pistol stowed but within reach. The strangers were four in number, three boys and a girl. They were in their mid-to-late teens, not much older than Grady, and they had brown skin that shined like petrified wood in the fading light. There was a single horse among them, frail and sickly, astride which sat the girl and the meanest looking of the boys. The other two boys walked alongside the horse with their hands thrust into the pockets of their trousers. They were all clean and well-dressed. Their faces were impassive, their eyes cruel. They came to a stop not ten yards from where Ellington stood, regarding him with cold, silent stares.

Bracing his hand against his horse's flank, Ellington tipped his hat and said, "Howdy there, young'uns." He smiled feebly, the corners of his mouth quivering.

The two boys beside the horse exchanged a glance. Nobody spoke. A low breeze rolled over the grass, rippling it like disturbed water. Ellington took a step forward, hooking his thumbs in his beltloops. He scanned the hills, where everything was still and quiet and cast in an ominous red-orange glow. "Y'all out here by your lonesome?" he asked.

The boy astride the horse looked down at the other two boys and then back at Ellington. He spat and looked around. "Nobody else is around here," he said. His English was clear but accented. To his friends, he said, "Por qué los americanos hacen preguntas tan tontas?" The others, including the girl, tittered like foxes and shook their heads, looking at Ellington with disdain.

Ellington's eyes narrowed and his mouth drew into a hard line. "Now, look here," he said. "Just 'cause I don't know what you's sayin' don't mean I don't know when I'm bein' made fun of. Where's your parents, anyhow?"

Their snickering subsided. The girl whispered something to the boy sitting in front of her on the horse, who was clearly the leader of the group. He nodded solemnly, swung his leg over the horse's neck, and hopped to the ground. Running his hand through his longish, sleek black hair, he grinned at Ellington and took several long strides forward, his head slightly tilted. "Why does it matter to you where are our parents?"

Ellington swallowed but remained rooted in place. "Don't matter none to me," he said. "Just askin', is all. These parts can be dangerous, so far from town."

The boy's grin widened and he advanced closer,

now just a few paces from Ellington. "Dangerous?" he said. "Who will make it dangerous for us? Are you—how you say—*threatening* us?"

"Ain't nobody makin' no such threats of any kind. Just, ah, lookin' out for ye, is all. Lots of things other'n me out here. Indians, and such." He gestured to the east and added, "And y'all know what they say about them hills out thataway."

The boy nodded slowly, taking another step closer and looking deep into Ellington's eyes. "Sí, gringo, I know what they say," he said quietly, almost whispering. "But I do not believe what they say. Do you, gringo? Do you believe these things they say?"

"Well, I don't rightly know what all I believe. But I know I don't aim to find out. I've never stuck around here much long after dark, in any case."

The boy nodded again. "Tell me, gringo, from where do you come?"

"Oh, got me a farm on the edge of town, not too—"

"No, gringo. Not where you live now. From where did you come before you come to California?"

Ellington tried to force a nervous little laugh, but it came out hoarse and awkward and it caught in his throat. He coughed into his fist and said, "Oh, er, right. I see what you mean. I'm a Texan, originally. Been in California goin' on two years, now."

Nodding and stroking his smooth, hairless chin, the boy said, "Texas. Claro, claro. I have never been to Texas. I and my friends have always been in California. We are as you gringos like to say, *Californios.*"

"Er, right. That's, ah, that's real good. Thanks for, er, sharin' your homeland with us, and all that."

Frowning, the boy said, "This is funny to me. It is funny because I did not choose to share it with you thieving americanos. None of us did, but you came and you took it."

Ellington chewed the inside of his cheek and shifted from one leg to the other, rubbing the fingers of his left hand with the thumb of his right. "Right, well. Least we got a whole lotta land to go around. And I, ah, I don't reckon the land was lawfully *yours* so a word like 'thievin'' don't hardly seem right."

The boy looked around. His eyes lingered on the rocks where Grady was hiding, but if he suspected anyone was there, he made no sign of it. When his gaze fell back upon Ellington, his eyes were black with malice and hate. "If the land was not mine, then why did you thank me for it?"

"Just somethin' to say, I guess. Bein' polite, is all. Now, much as I enjoy talkin', I really ought to be getting' on home."

The boy said nothing but clasped his hands behind his back and stepped around Ellington to examine his horse, peering into its eyes and lifting its chops to inspect its gums. Ellington watched him for a moment before glancing at the other three, who regarded him with the stony diffidence of old statues. The girl was slender and beautiful, with long, rolling waves of black hair and heavy-lidded, thick-lashed eyes full of a somber kind of mourning. One of the other boys was tall and looked enough like the leader that they were probably brothers, although he wasn't as handsome, and he lacked the leader's cool, relaxed swagger. The third boy was the shortest of the group and had lighter skin. He was painfully thin, and his hat was too big for him, drooping low over his brow and casting his face in shadow.

Ellington moved his gaze between the leader and the other three, fidgeting and quietly sucking on his teeth. He glanced over at the rocks, where there was no movement or indication that anyone was there. Another balmy breeze blew up from the south, gustier than the last, and his baggy trousers flapped against his legs.

The boy was circling Ellington's horse, patting and stroking it and whispering indecipherable things to it in Spanish. He came to a stop in front of Ellington, so close the tips of their noses were almost touching. A lizard lay poised on a nearby rock, watching with wide eyes, its neck pulsating. Overhead, a trio of buzzards circled though there was not yet anything dead to be seen.

In a flash of movement, the boy drew a Bowie knife from his belt and stuck its long blade deep into Ellington's stomach. The boy's expression remained hard and fixed even as the blood began to flow. Ellington cried out and leapt back, the blade sliding out of him. He clapped his hand over the wound and blood squirted between his fingertips, the stain blooming out across his shirt and spreading down his pantleg with the quickness of a contagion. Ellington fixed his attacker with wide eyes and a firmly set mouth, like he was both astonished and unsurprised by this assault. He opened his mouth but only blood came out, spraying a fine mist onto the boy's face. The boy did not flinch.

Ellington shuffled backward, staring at the boy for another moment before turning and loping awkwardly away from the road, brushing past disinterestedly grazing cattle and tripping over rocks and desert shrubbery. The trail of blood left in his wake looked black against the dirt.

"Are you going to let him escape, Felipe?" asked the short, thin boy, examining his fingernails. "Or should Ylario and I go after him?"

"Be calm, Martín," said Felipe. He took his handkerchief out of his back pocket and wiped his face.

"I am calm," said Martín. "I only want to know—"

"I will handle it," said Felipe. "He is mine to handle." He turned around and said, "Innocencia, please watch over my brother and Martín."

The girl on the horse nodded and smirked down at the other two boys. "Like I am their mother."

"You are not my mother," said Ylario, but when his eyes met Innocencia's, they lingered there. Something passed between them. Ylario quickly looked away and went to Ellington's horse so he could rummage through the saddle bags. He immediately found the pistol and held it up like a prize.

"Do not hurt yourself," said Felipe, taking the gun from his brother and sticking it in the waistband of his pants. "See what else you can find. I will not be long."

Ellington hadn't made it far, but he at least remained upright, though he was hunched over like an old man and limping like a cripple. Felipe caught up to him and shoved him face-first into the dirt. He rolled the dying man over with his boot and looked into his eyes.

"I d-didn't do . . . n-nothin' t-to . . . you," stammered Ellington.

Felipe looked out over the dusty landscape. A

jackrabbit sat on its haunches a few yards away, its face upturned and its nose wiggling like it could smell Felipe's intentions. Felipe watched it for a moment and then looked back down at Ellington and said, "Even with your last breath, you lie."

Felipe stabbed Ellington thirteen more times before returning to his companions.

Once the strangers had departed, Grady staggered out from behind the rocks. They had taken the horse, and now everything was silent save for the occasional lowing of the stray cattle. The sky had gone dark, and the only light came from the faint, far-off glow of the city, little more than a pale-yellow speck in the distance.

Stumbling over obstructions he couldn't see, Grady made his way over to the black shape lying on the ground. Even in the night, the violence done unto Ellington was apparent. His body was covered from the waist upward in deep punctures. A long slice ran along his belly, spilling various viscera in obscene, coiled loops. Blood and brain matter leaked from a wound in his forehead, above his right eye. A legion of flies swarmed over him, feasting and burrowing and nesting.

A single tear rolled down Grady's cheek, followed some moments later by another, and then there were no more. Hunkering down on one knee, he dipped his hands in his father's blood and streaked it across his face like war paint. He stood up and spat. There was nothing else for him to do but start walking westward toward the lights.

INTERLUDE 1
THE WRITER'S LAMENT

IT'S NOT A bad start to a novel. Perhaps not my best, but it'll do. For now, it will have to do. I push the keyboard drawer into the desk and stand up, rubbing my eyes and looking around my darkened study. The skeleton on the Dead Inside poster hanging on the wall looks like it's laughing at me. It's always laughing. Sometimes, I imagine it speaks to me. "You'll never be more than me," it'll say. "I'm what your readers want. I'm all your readers want."

My eyes drift to the Until the Sun poster—a better book than Dead Inside, truly—and then to the Along the Path of Torment poster—my best book. Those posters never say anything.

Opening the minifridge beside my desk, I take out a bottle of tonic water and pour three fingers into a tumbler. I light a cigarette and go to the window, looking out at the black hills studded with yellow and orange lights twinkling in the pre-dawn darkness. During the day, when the sun is high and hot, the view is much like the cover of Torment, and there's something I've always found hauntingly satisfying about that.

I sip my drink and look over my shoulder at my computer screen, at all those black words embedded in their stark white page.

"You're becoming a hack," says the Dead Inside skeleton. "You're selling out."

"Fuck off," I mutter, turning my back on the window and leaving the study, shutting the door behind me. I shuffle down the hall, trailing smoke, clutching my drink close to me like it means something. The hissing carbonation is crisp and loud in the otherwise silent condo.

I open the door to my bedroom and flick on the light, forgetting about the Cleveland girl in my bed. She stirs and sits up, her long blonde hair a wild mane around her head. I stare at her, momentarily dumbfounded by the burst bubble of my solitude. She blinks at me, eyes big and long-lashed, cloudy with sleep. "What time is it?" she asks, yawning.

"Almost five," I say, collapsing

into the armchair in the corner. I toss back the rest of the tonic water so I can ash into the glass. "What time is your flight?"

"You keep asking me that," she says, yawning a second time, stretching. "It's at ten-twenty."

"I'll get you a Lyft," I say, not looking at her. "I have things to do."

"What things?"

"I need to get some more writing done, and then I need to go tanning, and then I need to drive to San Diego."

I feel her eyes on me. "What's in San Diego that's more important than taking me to the airport? You didn't pick me up, either."

"Don't get sentimental. It doesn't suit you. Besides, I don't go to LAX unless I absolutely have to."

She sniffs. "Fine. Whatever. I'm not being sentimental. But I still want to know what's in San Diego."

I suck on the cigarette, my gaze lifting to the high ceiling. "A friend's book launch party. Book parties are a dying thing. So, when your friend has one, you go to it. Especially when your friend is one of the great writers of your generation."

"Gotcha." The feeling of her eyes on me is becoming unnerving. I wish

HUMAN-SHAPED FIENDS

I'd stayed in my study a while longer. "How long have you been up?"

I shrug. "All night. I didn't go to bed."

"You've been writing this whole time?"

"Trying to. I have to start making progress. I have a deadline. These months of false starts have finally caught up to me."

"When is it due?"

"Soon. Too soon."

"This is the cowboy thing, right?"

I snort. "Yeah, sure. The cowboy thing."

"I still don't know why you agreed to it. Cowboys really don't fit with your precious aesthetic." She enunciates "aesthetic" like it's a hairball.

"No," I say. "They don't. I suspect that might be why I'm struggling to find inspiration."

"There was a time when you said I inspired you. You said there were whole worlds inside me that you wanted to explore and transcribe. That a single night with me could give you endless pages of material."

Jesus, did I really say that? Yeah, probably. Sounds like something I'd say. I drop my cigarette into the glass, half-finished, and look at her, feeling very little. Feeling almost nothing. "I'm not seeing your point," I tell her.

She frowns. "Well, you've barely touched me all weekend. Maybe that's your problem. You've neglected your muse."

I lift the tumbler to my face, watching the half-smoked cigarette grow dark and soggy. Something about it makes me feel profoundly sad. "I haven't neglected you," I say. "You came three times."

"One of those was fake."

"Liar." I pause, thinking. "Which one?"

She looks away. "We used to spend whole weekends in bed." She sighs, and it sounds melodramatic, put-on. "I hate Los Angeles, you know. I really, really hate it. I only come out here for you."

I shut my eyes. "Sometimes, I hate it too."

"Yeah, well. You hate most things."

"I don't hate you," I offer noncommittally.

"What's your favorite thing about me?"

"Your ability to properly use semicolons."

"I can't tell if you're being serious or not."

"Neither can I, honestly."

She bites her lip. "I think next time you should come to Cleveland. I like you better in Cleveland."

I tell her that's fine, wondering if I care enough for there to be a next time.

CHAPTER 2

THE HOUR WAS late, and the moon was high and fat in the black sky when Grady arrived home. Tabitha, his mother, sat collapsed in a wicker chair in the small living room, listening in a weighted laudanum stupor as he gave her the news. When he was finished, she stared at him for a while with sleepy eyes and a slack face until she slowly drew herself to her feet and ambled to the cupboard to pour herself a glass of brandy. She downed it in two swallows and then stood there for a moment before pouring another glass for herself and one for Grady. She brought it to him, and he took it, staring into its amber depths. He cupped it with both hands and brought it to his lips as his mother watched him.

"Why you got blood on your face?" she asked him, her voice a soft murmur. "That his?"

Grady nodded. "I put it there," he said.

"Why'd you do that?"

Shrugging, Grady said, "Just somethin' to do."

Tabitha's head bobbed slowly. She sipped her brandy. "This . . . this maybe isn't such a terrible thing," she said.

HUMAN-SHAPED FIENDS

The corners of Grady's mouth twitched, turned down. "How's that?" He gripped his glass very tightly.

Tabitha went to the window and looked out at the night, holding her drink close to her chest. "We don't have to hide no more," she said after some time.

"No," Grady said, too loudly. "I done told you already. I'm through with all that."

"Keep your voice down. Your son is asleep."

Grady flinched. "Don't call him that."

"We don't have to hide no more," Tabitha said again. "It's what he is."

"He ain't. He's a monster."

"Shush now. He's not no monster."

"He's got three eyes, Ma. He eats mice and birds and such."

"Saves needin' a cat." Tabitha drained her glass and looked at her son. The moonlight exaggerated her still-youthful features, made her beautiful. "You can call me Tabby now. No use in pretendin'."

"Ain't gonna call you no such thing," Grady said.

Tabitha came to him and stroked his hair. She put her palm on the back of his head and pressed his face to her breasts, gasping a little. "Come to bed," she whispered. "Let's celebrate."

Grady grunted and withdrew himself from her embrace. "Ain't nothin' to celebrate. My pa is dead, and his killers is out there roamin' free. I gotta go to town and talk to the sheriff."

Tabitha nodded, her eyes vacant and hazy. "I know, baby, I know. But the sheriff'll still be there in the mornin'. Let me get you some tincture. It'll set your nerves at ease."

"I don't need that stuff like you do. You ought to lay off it. It makes you slow and stupid."

But Tabitha was already returning to the cupboard and taking out the dark brown bottle of laudanum and a silver tablespoon. She brought it over to Grady and poured the medicine into the spoon. "Open for the train," she said.

Grady glared at her for a few long seconds before submitting and opening his mouth. The spoon clicked against his teeth.

"That's my good boy. Now come to bed. I ache for you. I need you inside me."

Grady's head lolled. He blinked lazily. "I should . . . wash up first. I still got . . . his blood . . . "

"Nonsense, baby." Tabitha set the laudanum bottle down on the nearby table and hooked her fingers in her son's belt, tugging him toward her bedroom. "Leave it on. I rather like it."

Once Tabitha was asleep, sprawled on the bed in a pool of her own perspiration and with semen still drying on her bare chest, Grady got up and walked naked to the corner of the room where the creature slept in its crib. He stood swaying slightly, holding the sides of the crib for support and scowling down at the slumbering beast within it. Its mouth was open, exposing its sharp, gnarled teeth. Its long, forked tongue hung like a dog's against its pudgy cheek. It was clad in a blue onesie that—like all its clothes—was sewn with a kind of third pant leg, closed off at the end, to sheath the thing's enormously long penis.

HUMAN-SHAPED FIENDS

When the creature loped about in its awkward toddler's gait, its penis dragged along behind it like a dead snake affixed to its groin. It often tripped over it, and it would yowl and bleat in pain until Tabitha came cooing to its rescue, stroking its injured member while Grady and Jim looked on in disgust.

"I ought to kill you," Grady whispered, his speech slurry. "One day, I reckon I will."

The creature stirred—first, the eye on the left side of its forehead swung slowly open, followed by the two that were positioned normally. Its lips trembled into something like a smile, and it raised its clawed hands toward Grady. It grunted and then drew itself to its feet, hopping up and down and making a ghastly noise that might have been a giggle. Grady stepped back, out of the thing's reach. The crib rocked and creaked with the creature's excited bouncing. It had gotten much too big for the crib, but if they didn't keep it penned up at night, it would sneak out of the house to hunt vermin.

"Go back to sleep," Grady hissed. He cast a wary glance at his mother, but she was snoring lightly in her laudanum coma. Tears welled up in all three of the creature's eyes, and thick snot oozed from its pug-like nose. It kept looking from Tabitha to Grady, whipping its head back and forth with such force that its tangled black hair whipped about its head. It whined and blubbered, fingering the buttons on its onesie and tugging on its penis. "Fuck you want, you ugly bastard?" said Grady. The creature extended its arms toward Grady, opening and closing its chubby hands with their pointed black talons. Grady only sneered at it. "One day," he said. "One day I'll put an end to you."

INTERLUDE 2
YOU DON'T EVER GO FULL META

NCEST: CHECK.
Drug abuse: Check.
Damaged youth: Check.
What I'm doing is checking boxes, trying to fulfill whatever it is I think readers expect when they pick up a Chandler Morrison novel. Maybe it's entirely in my imagination, but I don't think it is.

"It's not," says the Dead Inside skeleton. "It's real. You know it's real. You're a brand. That's all you are."

It's so right I can't even bring myself to feel animosity toward it. At some point, I stopped being an artist and instead became a product. The worst part is, I can't quite pinpoint how much I care. I am unable to locate meaning. In anything.

The only thing to be done is shut

down my computer for the day and hit the tanning salon before Brian's book party. It's been nearly a week since I've gotten a tan, which is a problem for several reasons. Namely, I cannot be seen in public with my skin looking anything less than golden. There's also the tanning salon staff to think about. They're probably worried about my unexplained absence—I'm usually there daily—and I'm not one to make people worry. I am not a wholly selfish creature.

✽ ✽ ✽

The book launch party is for Brian Asman's latest novel, *Surfer Dudes from Hell . . . IN SPACE!* I read a galley copy and found it gripping and, at times, emotionally devastating.

The party is being held poolside at the Rancho Valencia Resort & Spa. I bump into Katy Perry in the lobby, who asks about my dog. I don't have a dog, but I tell her it's doing fine. She says we should do brunch soon, so I tell her to text me, but only because I'm pretty sure she doesn't have my number.

I find Brian smoking a joint next to a huge table stacked with copies of *Surfer Dudes from Hell . . . IN SPACE!* out by the pool, talking to Autumn

Christian. They spot me and wave me over.

"Yo, dude," Brian says, "Thanks for coming. Way cool of you."

"Yeah, no worries," I say, lighting a cigarette and looking around. There are substantially more people than there have been at any of my book launch parties. A DJ is playing a synth-mix of U2's "Even Better Than the Real Thing." There's even someone from Vogue and, I'm pretty sure, Rolling Stone. I didn't even think Rolling Stone was still in print. I have to suppress a wave of envy. "Congratulations, this is . . . quite a party."

"There are too many people," Autumn says. "I hate it." She looks apologetically at Brian and adds, "Or, um, what Chandler said."

"Thanks, guys," Brian says. "Far out." He squints at me. "One question, though, dude—why are you dressed like a cowboy?"

He's referring to my wide-brimmed Stetson, rawhide vest, and long black duster. I don't think he's referring to the cowboy boots because I'm always wearing cowboy boots, even when I'm not dressed like a cowboy. "Oh, this," I say, looking down at my outfit and fingering the brim of my hat. "Method writing. Trying to get in character. Writing this Western has been a real struggle."

"Right on, dude, right on." He hits the joint. "Is it working?"

"Hard to say. I'm sort of struggling with the narrative. And I'm writing it from a third-person objective point of view, which is . . . difficult. I like the effect—very cold, very detached, which is kind of my thing—but there's this, like, constant pull I have to keep fighting, because I want to automatically jump to a single character's point of view in any given scene."

"Objective POV is tough," Autumn says, nodding sympathetically.

"I'm thinking about going meta with it," I say.

Brian's face becomes serious. "Dude," he says, "hold up. How meta are we talking here?"

"Like, all-the-way meta. Charlie-Kaufman-in-Adaptation meta. Self-insertion and everything. A whole subplot about me—or, I guess, more of a parody of me—as I struggle to write this book. I think it might help me break through the barrier I've been up against. Plus, autofiction is all the rage these days."

Brian purses his lips and shakes his head. "I don't know, dude. Charlie Kaufman can go full meta, but the rest of us? That's risky business. Unless you're Charlie Kaufman, you don't ever go full meta."

"Yeah, no, I don't think that's fair," I say. "What about Martin Amis? DFW? Nabokov, Murakami? How about Stephen King? Even Bret Easton Ellis did it in *Lunar Park*."

"*Lunar Park* is a good book," says Autumn.

Brian shakes his head. "The problem," he says, hitting his joint, "is only one of those examples writes horror. You're a horror author citing literary authors. Metafiction doesn't really lend itself to horror."

"I'm not a horror author," I say bristling a little. "I'm a satirist."

Brian strokes his beard. "Aren't you contracted to write a horror Western?"

"I'm contracted to write a Western with lots of blood, a high body count, and some supernatural elements. Nothing says it has to be horror."

"That, ah, sounds like horror to me. Besides, DHP specializes in horror."

"They specialize in dark fiction. They've published two of my last three books, and none of them were horror."

HUMAN-SHAPED FIENDS

Raising an eyebrow, Brian says, "Dead Inside isn't horror?"

"No. It's not. It's satire."

"What about Until the Sun?"

"Same deal."

"Until the Sun has vampires in it, dude," Autumn points out.

"Not, like, real vampires," I correct her.

"Still," says Brian, "it's not advisable, this whole meta thing. I mean, like, how are you going to work the 2020 shitshow into it? You're going to have to at least mention Covid."

"Fuck that, and fuck Covid. I mean, don't get me wrong—I take it very seriously, and I'm all about doing my part to stay the fuck home and mask up and all that, but the thing is, Covid doesn't fit with my aesthetic at all. People walking around with their masks hanging off their faces? No way. Chin-diapers have no place in a Chandler Morrison novel."

Autumn says, "I love it when you talk about yourself in third-person."

"I'm serious," I say. "People expect certain things from my work. Covid is one entire fashion faux pas that one hundred percent does not belong in my meticulously curated fictional universe."

"Are we going to be in it?" Autumn asks.

"I haven't decided yet. Probably. You're cool enough."

"Gnarly," says Brian.

"Yeah," I say, looking at the still, shimmering water of the pool. "Gnarly."

CHAPTER 3

SHERIFF BARTON STOOD fidgeting in the examination room of Dr. Druse's huge hillside manor while the physician packed his purchases—codeine, morphine, laudanum, syringes, and cocaine-infused lozenges and chewing gum—into a paper sack.

"How have the headaches been?" Druse asked, rolling the top of the bag closed and handing it to Barton.

Barton shrugged one shoulder. "Not so bad," he said. "The tincture helps." He took out his wallet and handed the doctor a wad of bill notes, which Druse pocketed so quickly it was as if the transaction had never even occurred.

Druse nodded, studying Barton closely from behind his horn-rimmed glasses. "Yes, I'd imagine it should. You look thin. How often have you been visiting that opium den?"

Barton shifted on his feet. "No more'n usual," he said. "Just every now and again."

Druse sucked his teeth. "Well, as long as it's not *too* often. Opium can be dangerous when inhaled. Intravenous use is much safer. And Orientals carry all sorts of foul diseases."

"I always make sure I don't touch any of 'em."

Clucking his tongue and shaking his head, the doctor said, "That'll keep you relatively safe from bacterial infection, because bacteria have limited mobility. But viruses have wings and can fly great distances."

"I'll keep that in mind," said Barton, nodding solemnly.

Druse led Barton out of the exam room and to the front door. They stepped out onto the porch and stood looking down at the dark rooftops below while the crickets chirped and a pack of wolves howled from somewhere far off. "It's nice out here," Barton said. "Peaceful."

"It is. I'm going to miss it."

"You goin' somewhere?"

"I am. I've been corresponding with a businessman in Ohio. Fellow by the name of Preston. He's interested in building a hospital, says he wants me to run it. I'll be on my way before the new moon, if all goes according to plan." He saw the look on Barton's face and laughed, clapping him on the back. "Fear not, Sheriff, there's a very good doctor on the other side of town I'll set you up with. He'll supply you with everything you need to keep your multitudinous ailments at bay."

Barton took a cigarette from his breast pocket and put it between his lips. He struck a match, cupping his hand around the hissing flame and touching it to the end of the cigarette. "Never figured you'd leave Los Angeles," he said, flicking the extinguished match into the dark. "It's more a place you come to. A last stop."

"You idealize it too much." The doctor walked off

the porch with his hands in his pockets. He kicked lightly at the dirt with the toe of his shoe. He looked up at Barton, the starlight shining in the lenses of his glasses. "The very soil here is poisonous. I've been to many places, Sheriff, but none that felt so diseased and corrupt as this."

Barton, his brow creased and his mouth drawn, puffed on his cigarette. "I don't know," he said. "Sometimes, I feel like that, too. Most times, I reckon. But there are other times when it's somethin' else. When it's a place of promise." He said this, but his voice lacked surety, like he doubted the words even as he spoke them.

"You're just buying into the illusion. It's a desert mirage. A dream of water in a vast expanse of dry dereliction and waste. You'll find no sustenance here, Sheriff. As a matter of fact, *you* should leave, too, while you still have your wits about you. You've got family money, right? I know you're not living in that fancy hotel on a sheriff's salary alone."

Barton looked away. "Jill had money," he said. "It was left to me when she passed."

"If I were you, I'd take that money and go somewhere nice. Somewhere better, where you can make a difference. I know you're beholden to your sense of duty, but nothing you do here will make any difference. You're up against something bigger than you. Bigger than anyone."

Barton slunk into the hotel lobby like a guilty thief, flinching at the chime of the bell above the door and squinting against the harsh light of the overhead chandelier. He took off his hat and pushed back his matted hair. The night clerk at the front desk bade him a "Most pleasant evening, Mr. Barton," a cheery lilt in his voice, his eyes twinkling behind his half-moon spectacles. Barton grunted and nodded before shuffling across the confounding pattern of the lush carpet and advancing up the stairs to the third floor. He let himself into his room, freshly made up and with a new bottle of gin resting on the nightstand like an answered prayer.

Unstrapping his gun belt and hanging it and his hat on the back of the door, he crossed the room and unscrewed the bottle, drinking straight from its mouth. He winced at the first swallow, but not the second or third or fourth. Wiping his mouth with the back of his hand, he went to the window and drew back the curtain, looking down at the street. Across from the hotel stood the Scarlet Macaw, its windows alight. Mirthful music drifted out from its entrance. Drunken men loitered outside, flirting with whores. Caroline was among them, laughing too hard at something a fat man was whispering to her. The light from the streetlamps made her straw-yellow hair glow like fire. Barton grimaced and turned away from the window.

Silver eyes stared out at him from beneath the bed, shining and unblinking. Two bony arms, the skin upon them mottled and white like curdled milk, reached out from the darkness. The long black fingernails scraped against the polished wood of the floor. A head emerged, its hair stringy and clotted with dirt, its visage pitted with holes chewed by subterranean vermin. The body and legs came next, clad in a frayed and filthy wedding dress. The creature rose to its feet, its joints popping like roasted corn kernels.

"Evenin', Jill," Barton said. "You're up early tonight."

"You gonna pour me some of that there?" she asked, gesturing to the bottle in Barton's hand.

"Wouldn't be good for you. I tell you that every night."

"One of these nights you'll change your mind."

"Don't reckon I will."

Jill moved past him, moving with the jerky, put-upon movements of a clumsily manipulated marionette. She peered out the window. "Your girl looks busy this evening. Does it hurt you to see it?"

"She's not my girl. She's not anybody's girl."

"You wish she was yours."

"Doesn't matter what I wish."

She came up behind him and put her arms around his narrow waist. "You're getting so thin," she whispered into his ear. He shivered. Her spider-like fingers crept up his torso and unbuttoned his shirt. Icy fingers massaged his chest. "You been spending more time with those Orientals, smoking their wicked flower?"

"No more time than usual."

"I don't *believe* you." She nibbled at his ear with her chipped gray teeth. "I just don't know why I can't be enough for you. Why you gotta try and find love in the arms of a whore and in the false pleasures of a drug." She moved her hand out of his shirt and reached down to squeeze his groin. "I got all the love you need right here."

"You're dead, Jill. You're gone."

"I *am* dead. I'm *not* gone."

"It's not my fault what happened to you."

"I wish you'd leave this devil town. We can go tonight, just you and me. We can go back home. Our house is still there, you know. It's been taken over by snakes and spiders and dogs, but we can take it back. It can be ours again."

"I belong here, Jill. I have a responsibility to the people of this town."

Jill withdrew from him and hobbled to the bed, tossing her hair. "Oh, yes, the big *sheriff* has *responsibility*." She stretched out atop the covers, plucking a centipede dangling from her nostril and plopping it into her mouth. Staring at him as she chewed, she said, "They don't respect you, *Sheriff Barton*. They see you for what you are. A pretty boy from Oklahoma who's too weak and wasted to keep them safe from themselves."

"That's not so."

"There's a reckoning coming, Sheriff. It's coming real soon. You can't stop it. All you can do is wait and watch or leave and never look back. But you can't stop it."

Barton pulled from the bottle and didn't say anything.

"Come to bed, James. Lie with me for a while. You can decide what you're gonna do in the morning."

"There's not anythin' to decide," said Barton, but he got into bed with his dead wife all the same.

Interlude 3
David Lynch's Car
Commercial

AUTUMN DRIVES UP from San Diego to have coffee with me at Intelligentsia. We're sitting at an outside table, smoking cigarettes despite the spiteful glares of the other patrons. The most recent pages of my manuscript lay before her, weighted down against the light breeze with her lighter and pack of Camels.

"I don't like that you made me a smoker in your book," Autumn says, hitting her cigarette. "I've never been a smoker."

"Everyone smokes in my books," I say. "It's, like, a *thing*. Anyway, that's not important. What do you think of the rest of it? I was hoping you could diagnose my nagging case of writer's block."

She looks at the pages stacked on the table. "Your problem," she says,

"I think, is the setting. It's hard to do your usual thing in a Western world, where everything is dirty and grimy."

"My . . . usual thing? What's my usual thing?"

"You know. The whole, like . . . glamorpunk schtick, where everyone is rich and pristine and attractive."

Nodding slowly, I push my Persol sunglasses up the bridge of my nose and glance at my Versace wristwatch. "Glamorpunk," I say, testing the word in my mouth, tasting it. "I like that." I drag contemplatively from my cigarette. "So, how do I . . . fix it? How do I write the glamorpunk aesthetic into a Western world?"

Autumn looks at the manuscript and flicks ash onto the ground beside her. She sighs heavily. "I don't know that you can. Not *this* world, at least. Not with this story. From what you've told me about it, where you're going with it . . . it's just not that type of book. The Western part, at least. You can do whatever you want with the meta parts, I guess. Every scene you put yourself into will get it by default." She scowls at my outfit. "I mean, Jesus, you're like a walking Versace ad."

"Thank you," I say.

HUMAN-SHAPED FIENDS

"It wasn't a compliment, but I'm not surprised you took it as one."

"The blazer isn't Versace," I confess. "It's Hugo Boss. I have a Versace blazer but my friend's cat clawed a hole in it."

"I don't care what brand your blazer is," Autumn says, sounding exhausted. "But for God's sake, Chandler, it has *sequins*."

"What's wrong with sequins?"

"Forget it. I'm not sure how your publisher will feel about the whole autofiction element, though. Have you told them yet?"

I look away. "No. I'm, ah . . . a bit anxious about it. They've been amazing to work with, and they've been good to me—Jarod, especially—and I'm afraid of what they might say when I turn in something that's not exactly what I pitched them." I notice a girl sitting a few tables away reading a Joan Didion paperback. She looks familiar. I wonder idly if I've slept with her. When she glances in my direction, I turn my attention back to Autumn and continue, "It's not . . . *not* what I pitched them. It's just got . . . an unexpected twist."

"I mean, it's not like they can really be surprised by whatever you end up handing in. Asking you to do a

Western is like asking David Lynch to do a car commercial. So, like, I'm sure on some level they knew what they were getting into."

I think for a moment, then take out my phone and tap a quick note to myself. "I like that," I say. "The bit about David Lynch doing a car commercial. I'm going to use that."

"Just make sure you credit me."

"Wouldn't dream of doing otherwise."

CHAPTER 4

GRADY SAT RED-EYED and haggard in front of Sheriff Barton's desk the next morning, wearily recounting his father's murder while Barton rolled a cocaine lozenge around in his mouth. Deputy Chuck Conrad stood leaning against the wall with his feet crossed at the ankles and his arms folded over his chest. He had a cigarette tucked behind his ear, poking out from the sweaty tangles of his curly black hair. Jake Farrington, a reporter for the town newspaper, sat in a chair toward the back corner of the room, scribbling notes on a long roll of parchment.

Barton leaned back in his chair and stared out the window for a long time after Grady stopped talking. He lit a cigarette, absently offering one to the boy, who declined. When Barton finally spoke, his voice was scratchy and tired. "These kids," he said, "you recognize any of 'em?"

"Only two of 'em," said Grady. "The one with the knife, we was in the same class a year or so back. Felipe is his name. Alvitre, I think. His brother is Ylario. They's both Californios. Everybody knows about 'em, but they don't go to the school no more."

"Why's that?"

"They done got kicked out after they set a boy's hair on fire."

Farrington emitted a gleeful squeal. Conrad shot him a reproachful glare. Barton said, "They give any reason for doin' a thing like that?"

"Yes, sir. They said it was on account of the boy was too white."

Farrington hooted, writing faster.

Barton nodded and bit down on his lozenge. "Well, we best ride on out there and have a look. Chuck, you can get with Avery when we get back, draw up some posters." To Grady, he said, "You able to lead the way?"

The three men and the boy stood in a loose half-circle with their hats in their hands around the corpse of Jim Ellington, the hot sun lording above them like a cruel master. Their horses snuffled and pawed at the dirt with their hooves. A legion of buzzards, scared away by their approach, hovered overhead and waited for them to leave.

It was Conrad who spoke first. "It was fiends that did this," he said, holding his bandana over his mouth and nose, shaking his head at the body. "Fiends in human shape."

"Say," said Farrington, "that's pretty good. I might have to use that."

Barton drew his handkerchief to his face and knelt by the corpse, examining it as he swatted flies away from his head. Much of the flesh on Ellington's face had been picked off by the birds. Maggots squirmed in his exposed guts like tiny wriggling fingers, beckoning to him. "I count fourteen knife wounds," he said.

"Fiends," Conrad said again.

"Fiends, indeed," said Barton, rising from his haunches. He dashed sweat from his forehead with his handkerchief. "We best get him back to town. No good leavin' him for the buzzards." He eyed the large black birds with visible contempt. "After that, I'll be wantin' to speak with these boys' parents. The Alvarez boys."

"Alvitre," said Grady, looking up at the harsh, cloudless blue sky. "That's their name. Not Alvarez. Alvitre."

Barton glanced in the boy's direction and nodded. "Sure, yeah. Alvitre. Any case, we'll talk to the parents. See if we can scare up somethin' about who the other two with 'em might be, and where they might be headed."

"The gallows is where they're headed," said Conrad. He put a tentative hand on Grady's shoulder. "You all right, son?" His voice came out strained, awkward. Conrad was no more than a few years older than the boy, and the paternal affect didn't suit him.

Grady lowered his gaze from the sky, fixing his eyes on one of the buzzards, narrowing them as though he'd zeroed in on a target. "I am," he said. "I will be."

It was nearly dusk by the time Barton rode upon the Alvitre homestead. Conrad and Farrington were still with him. Grady had gone home in accordance with the sheriff's orders.

The cabin was well-built and impressive in size, seated in a wide valley among the hills some miles northeast of town. Laundry hung from a clothesline out front, flapping like flags in the breeze. Shadows pooled along the edges of the house. No sounds came from within.

"You gonna knock, Sheriff?" Conrad asked, shifting in his saddle.

Barton tipped his hat back and scanned the premises. Nothing moved. All was quiet save for the yipping of coyotes in the distance. He straightened and cleared his throat. "*Señor Alvitre*," he yelled out. "*This is Sheriff Barton. I'm here about your boys.*"

"Are you *certain* that's the best *idea*?" Farrington hissed. "He *might* be *dangerous*."

"If he's dangerous," said Barton, "we'll deal with him."

Slowly, the front door opened. A tall, lithe woman emerged. Her complexion was dark, her hair darker. A sudden gust of wind swept her long, white dress around her. She did not come down from the front step. "Qué es lo que quieres?" she called to Barton.

Barton edged his horse closer. Farrington and Conrad remained behind. "You speak English?" he asked.

"No inglés," the woman said.

Barton spat. "I think you're lyin'," he said. "Where's your husband?"

The woman looked long and hard into Barton's

eyes. The muscles of her face were taut and unmoving. "No inglés," she said again.

Not taking his eyes from the woman, Barton called back to the reporter, "Farrington, get on up here." Farrington pushed his horse up next to Barton's. "Ask this woman where her husband is," Barton said.

"Hell, Sheriff, my Spanish isn't quite as good as it used to be," Farrington said. "Ah, shit. Um, donde . . . marido?"

The woman glared with slitted eyes at Farrington. "Por qué estás aquí?"

"What'd she say?" asked Barton.

"She wants to know why we're here."

"Tell her . . . tell her that her boys are missin' and we want to know when she and her husband saw 'em last."

"Sus hijos . . . um, desaparecidos?" Farrington said. "Cuándo los vio por vez . . . última?"

The woman said nothing. She knotted her hands in front of her, rubbing them anxiously. She looked over her shoulder into the darkness of the house, said something low and unintelligible, and then removed herself from the doorway, out of sight.

"I don't like this," said Farrington.

"Just be ready to—" Barton started to say, but then his eyes flicked toward the rifle barrel sticking out the window. The muzzle flashed. The bullet struck Farrington's horse in the neck. It exited trailing a long jet of blood that splattered loudly on the dry, dead earth. The horse collapsed, crushing one of Farrington's legs beneath it. Farrington cried out. Barton drew his pistol and fired three successive shots into the window. The glass fell away, tinted scarlet with sprayed blood. A man's animal cry of agony rose from the house. The woman emerged again, dashing forth with a lunatic's sneer painted sloppily on her face. She had a meat cleaver raised above her head. Barton shot her between the eyes. A freshet of brain-spangled blood belched from the back of her head in a vulgar sneeze.

After a few moments, the wailing from the house died off. The atmosphere fell into an uneasy silence once again.

"Fuck," said Farrington. "I think my leg's broken."

Barton looked at him. He spat. "Conrad, take a look inside the house," he said to his deputy. "See if there's anythin' useful. Don't expect there will be. I'll tend to the writer."

CHAPTER 5

THE BATWING DOORS swung on creaky hinges as Felipe and his companions entered. A dusky orange lamplight cast the interior of the saloon in a hearthy glow. The weathered faces of its patrons swiveled toward the newcomers upon their arrival, observing them with bland indifference before sinking back into their separate solitudes, brooding over their ales and whiskeys. A tabby cat with tangled, matted fur lounged across an empty, lopsided table, licking its paws. A lone whore sat on the floor near the back, her thin legs spread out before her as she nursed a tall glass of liquor. Her mascara ran in long black tracks down her cheeks and her skimpy clothes were tattered and frayed.

Nobody was speaking. The bartender leaned against the counter, his sweaty hair hanging in his eyes as he polished a beer stein with a filthy white rag. The oily cloth squeaked loudly against the chipped glass.

The newcomers stood in a line near the entrance, not moving, their faces stern. They scanned the premises through heavy-lidded eyes. "I count six," said Martín in a low voice.

"That is including the whore," said Felipe. "And she does not count."

"Aim true," said Ylario.

The bartender glanced over at them again. He did not speak, but he raised a quizzical eyebrow and grunted. The drinker nearest him, a stout man in a ten-gallon hat and mud-stained overalls, wiped his mouth and stood up. He glared at the four strangers from beneath the shadow of his hat brim. His big, gnarled hand hovered near his holstered pistol. The other patrons in the bar started to pay attention, their glassy eyes gaining some degree of focus while their bodies remained inert. Even the cat sat up, stretching and looking at the man in the overalls with its huge gold eyes.

"Either buy a drink or don't," said the man in the overalls. His voice was surprisingly soft and high for someone of his stature. "But if you got somethin' to say, say it in English so we can all hear it. And stop standin' 'round like you're casin' the joint."

"You heard us," said Felipe in English. "But if you did not understand us, this is not our concern."

"If you are going to do this," Ylario said to Felipe, not in English, "do it now."

Innocencia crossed the room, her dress swirling around her legs, and sat down at the table upon which the cat was perched. She took the animal in her arms and began to stroke it. It meowed once and began to purr, nuzzling its face against her hand.

The whore had risen shakily to her feet. She wobbled over to an old man sitting at the end of the bar and began to whisper in his ear. Her gaze stayed glued to Felipe. The old man shook his head and shoved the whore away. She stumbled to the floor, spilling her drink. Her glass cracked on the dirty, knotted wood but did not break. It rolled away from her and came to a stop against the wall. She sat up and looked longingly after the glass, silently weeping.

"I guess maybe your friend didn't hear me right," the man in the overalls said to Felipe. "If you're goin' to say somethi—"

Felipe's hand shot behind him and drew Ellington's big revolver from his waistband. Holding it in both hands, he leveled the gun at the man in the overalls, thumbed back the hammer, and fired. The man's hat flew off and the top left quadrant of his head disappeared in a dark shower of red and pink gore. The man took two staggering steps forward before crumpling face-first into a heap on the floor, his wide ass sticking absurdly in the air. The old man at the end of the bar started to stand, reaching for a repeater that was leaning next to him, but Felipe squeezed off a second round that caught him in the throat. Blood ejaculated onto the bar in a spurting fountain. He swatted at the wound as though it were a bothersome mosquito, drawing his hand away and looking at the blood upon it with round, unbelieving eyes. He fell onto his side near the whore, who screamed and crab-walked backward, shrinking against the wall and clutching her knees to her chest.

The bartender had procured a shotgun from beneath the counter and was aiming it at Felipe. Felipe dove forward and Ylario and Martín both ducked right as the shotgun's barrel boomed. The batwing doors blew off their hinges, sending splinters of wood flying. Felipe kicked over a table and crouched behind it. The bartender pointed his gun at the table and squeezed the trigger, only to be met with the dry click of a misfire. He cursed, and Felipe rose from cover and shot him in the mouth. Blood and teeth and shredded bits of bone and muscle splattered onto the countertop. The barkeeper reeled back into the rows of liquor bottles behind him, knocking them off their shelves and slumping to the floor as they fell and shattered around him.

The remaining men were reaching for their pistols when Felipe gunned them down—one caught a bullet in the eye, the back of his head blossoming like a flower, and the other was hit just below his nose, turning the bottom of his face into a ghastly gash from which blood shot and thin tendrils of smoke plumed.

Felipe lowered the gun. "Take what weapons and food you can find," he said to his companions. "We may be on the road a long time."

Martín was walking toward where the whore sat crouched and shivering, black tears streaming from her eyes. He unbuckled his belt. "Give me a minute alone with the lady, first," he said.

Wordlessly, the others exited the saloon and waited.

As they were riding back to town, with Conrad holding an incessantly groaning Farrington upright in his saddle, they came upon the ravaged saloon. The whore sat outside, an unlit cigarette between her trembling fingers. Her eyes stared into nothing visible to man.

HUMAN-SHAPED FIENDS

The riders halted. Barton dismounted and told Conrad to stay with Farrington, and then he spoke in hushed tones with the whore for several minutes before going inside. He did not remain there long.

"What is it?" Conrad asked when Barton returned to the horses.

"A massacre," Barton said. He drew a bottle of gin from his saddlebag and took a long pull. "Same crew we're after, by the sounds of it. The whore's description of 'em matches the boy's."

"Did she see where they went?" asked Conrad.

"She did not."

"Take me inside," said Farrington.

"No need for that," said Barton.

"Sheriff, with all due *respect*, I'm a *journalist*. I keep the good people of this town *informed*. There is absolutely a *need*."

Barton spat. "All right," he said. "But I don't want anythin' sensational. No need to cause a panic."

CHAPTER 6

BARTON STOOD IN the cramped little room on the second floor of the Scarlet Macaw several nights later, a stench of alcohol and opium smoke rising from his pores as he undressed. His eyelids drooped and his shoulders sagged. A copy of the town paper lay on the bureau. The front-page headline blared "HUMAN-SHAPED FIENDS LOOSE IN LOS ANGELES." It stared at Barton like an accusation.

Caroline, already naked, watched him from the bed. "You look worse every time I see you," she said. There was no concern in her voice. It was a statement of observation. Her tone betrayed no lament. "And it ain't even been that long since I last saw you. Pretty soon they're gonna need to come up with a new name for you, *pretty boy.*"

Barton stepped out of his trousers. His long body was scrawny, white, and shivering. He joined Caroline in the bed, drawing her to him for warmth, though the room was not cold. "As long as I'm still pretty enough for you, I don't care what they call me."

"Got nothin' to do with bein' pretty and everythin' to do with bein' rich. Rich *enough*, at least."

Barton hushed her, pressing his forehead to hers

and stroking her flaxen hair with his quivering fingers. He searched her eyes as though they contained something lost.

"Why you always gotta *do* this, James?" Caroline said. She sounded impatient and irritated, but she did not move. "Why you always want to lie here like we're lovers?"

Barton pulled her closer, burying his face in her hair, taking in the scent of her. He ran his hand over her smooth back, up over her shoulder, down the length of her slender arm. He took her hand in his, twining his fingers between hers. "Who says we aren't lovers?" he asked in a sleepy whisper.

"I do, for starters. You're nothin' but a customer."

"I do love it when you sweet-talk me."

"I'm *serious*, James. I think things'll be a whole lot easier for you if you just wake up and realize that."

Barton's brow knitted. His pale lips thinned. "Easier how?" he asked. Almost as a weak, hurt-sounding afterthought, he added, "I'm awake."

"You ain't."

"Easier how, Caroline?" he asked again. "What do you mean by all that?"

"I *mean*, Sheriff, that I don't reckon there's an able-bodied man in this town I ain't been to bed with at least once, and they all talk."

Barton winced. "I don't want to hear about what your other suitors have to say when they're with you."

Caroline rolled her eyes and sat up, folding her arms over her chest. "They *ain't* suitors, James. They're customers. Just like you. And a lot of 'em talk about *you*. There's a whole lotta violence in this town.

A whole lotta death. People are startin' to think maybe you ain't the man for your job."

Barton closed his eyes, rolling over on his back and clasping his hands behind his head. He sighed heavily. "I don't see what that's got to do with me and you."

"There *is* no me and you, James," said Caroline, her voice softening. "And I think if you came to terms with that instead of mopin' around about it, maybe you could focus more on cleanin' up this town. If I was you, I'd start with BIPOC Alley. Nothin' good goes on there. Burn it all down, I say."

Opening one eye and pointing it at Caroline, Barton said, "It's all a lot more complicated than you think. Than anyone thinks. It's got nothin' to do with me or the matters of my heart. There's politics involved."

"Well, whatever you want to call it." Caroline shrugged. "You best figure it out, anyhow. How 'bout that dead cattle rancher from a few days back? His son was drinkin' in here last night, you know. And the paper says the massacre at that saloon some miles east is related. Nasty business."

"I'm workin' on it."

"I mean, it ain't nothin' to me. I don't got to worry about *my* job. As long as there are men, there'll be whores."

"You could say the same for violence. For death."

"You could, I reckon. Now, are you gonna fuck me, or are we gonna just set here talkin'?"

"No more talk," said Barton. "Just lie with me awhile. Just lie with me."

CHAPTER 7

AFTER SEVERAL DAYS of traveling through the desert, the Alvitre gang came to a high hill rising from the road. It was pocked with palm trees and had a cave near its summit. On the other side of the road was a well. Felipe dismounted his horse and went to the well. He placed his hands on its lip and looked down. He picked up the rope-affixed tin pail lying in the dirt and sniffed it, and then he tossed into the well where it landed at the bottom with a splash. Taking hold of the rope, he drew the pail back up and brought it to his lips. The water was crisp and fresh. He wiped his mouth and looked to the cave at the top of the hill. To his companions, he said, "This is where will stay for now."

Two years earlier, before they were killers and everything started to get confused, Felipe and Innocencia sat huddled close together atop a blanket on a grassy hill one warm, bright, summer afternoon while a wagon train ambled along beneath them, some hundred yards out. The fingers on Felipe's left hand were entwined with those on Innocencia's right. The hot sun ignited Innocencia's hair like glittering onyx, but Felipe was not looking at her hair. He was watching the wagon train, and his eyes were slitted with hate.

"I do not like to see it," he said after a while. "They keep coming and I do not like to see them come. I wish they would stay away."

"As long as there is land, they will come," said Innocencia. She plucked a dandelion from beside the blanket and held it before her face, twirling it between her fingertips. "Los Angeles to them is a place of great promise."

"Maybe it was once, before they polluted it."

"Maybe they see us as the pollution. Things are different depending on who you are and from where you come. Nothing is the same to anyone. There are only perspectives."

"I do not believe that. Everything is one way. Nature is a law. There are no interpretations."

Innocencia tucked the dandelion behind her ear and pointed at a small boy running alongside the wagon train with a cheerfully bounding terrier. As the dog ran, its fur billowing and its ears cocked back and its tongue hanging out the side of its mouth, it never took its eyes off the boy for more than a second or two. "Do you see that dog? With the little boy? The dog does not care about what the boy may grow up to be. That boy may become a murderer or a rapist, but the dog only sees the boy as he is now. Innocent and perfect. Uncorrupted. Maybe we should all learn to see as dogs. Maybe then there wouldn't be so many murderers, so many rapists. Maybe people grow into what we expect them to be."

HUMAN-SHAPED FIENDS

Felipe shook his head. "That dog is just a dumb animal. It does not know any better. We do."

"Do we? What do you know of that boy? How do you know he will not be a great hero, or even simply a good man?"

"I know," said Felipe, "because there are no good white men."

Barton stood with the mayor in the parlor of his mansion, the two men staring at the hulking Person with Disabilities in the cage. It was nearly seven feet tall. Its naked, shit-streaked body was rippled with what seemed like equal amounts fat and muscle. Drool hung from its chin as it gawked through the bars at its onlookers. The mayor was beaming. He ran his hands through his oiled-back silver hair and nodded appreciatively. "Best purchase I ever made," he said. "Anyone who says money can't buy happiness obviously doesn't have any."

Barton scratched his jaw. "What do you use it for?" he asked.

The mayor snorted. "What do you *think* I use it for? Fucking, James, *fucking*."

"You . . . fuck this creature?"

"Of course not. *It* fucks *me*. Its cock may not look like much, but when it's aroused . . . " He whistled, grinned. "Granted, *I* attempted to fuck *it*, but it damn near killed me for trying. It's very particular about what you put in its asshole."

"Most men are."

"It's not a *man*, Sheriff. I can't keep the damned

thing from lathering itself with its own feces every few hours. And I hardly *feed* it." He lit a cigar. "I've got a few others I keep locked in a room upstairs I use for the same purpose, but none of them are as big or as beautiful as this brute." He grinned at Barton, curls of smoke seeping from between his too-large teeth. "You want to see them?"

"I'll pass. Your secretary said you wanted to see me."

"Yes, yes. Come, we'll go in another room, away from the stink. I need to put it upstairs with the others, and I will, but for now I just like looking at it." He gave the Person with Disabilities a final glance of longing admiration before leading Barton into a wide, well-lit sitting room. Barton took a seat in a plush armchair and the mayor poured him a glass of cognac from behind the bar. Barton sipped it, watching the mayor, waiting.

Leaning against the wall, puffing on his cigar, the mayor sighed and said, "James, I don't think you've quite figured out how things work."

"I don't follow."

"There's a certain . . . code. There are things—key, specific things—that make this town run the way it does. Our job as civil appointees is to make sure those things continue to operate smoothly. Sometimes we need to help them along, but most times we just need to stay out of the way. Los Angeles is a machine. All we have to do, mainly, is keep the gears oiled and just . . . let it run. Do you understand what I'm saying?"

"Not really, sir. No, I don't reckon I do."

The mayor sighed again. "Take BIPOC Alley, for instance. I know you and your deputy have been rousting up some Black and Indigenous People of Color down there, and frankly, I'd like for it to stop. I told you before that you needed to ease up on the shootings down there, and you did, but now the rest of it has to stop, too. No more police activity. None whatsoever."

"We go where the crime is. There's a lot of crime down there."

"Yes, naturally, it's a hotbed of it. But it's *good* crime, James. It's the crime we *need*. The Black and Indigenous People of Color take care of themselves. More often than not they just kill and rape each other. It's only when they start killing and raping white folk that we need to step in."

INTERLUDE 4
ANACHRONISMS

THE CLEVELAND GIRL calls me the day after I've sent her the latest bit of the book. I'm lying naked on my balcony, letting the sun dry the last damp remnants of spray tan solution on my skin. I light a cigarette before answering.

"This is so incredibly stupid," she says. "You have characters in the Old West referring to Black people as 'Black and Indigenous People of Color.' That's a twenty-first century term. It doesn't make any sense and it sounds silly."

I suck on the cigarette, my eyes drifting from the cityscape beneath me to the long, slender angles of my body. I am taken by its beauty. My body's, not the city's.

"It's an anachronism," I say, a shrug in my voice. "I see no reason why I should have to conform to the racist terminology of the times. It's *my* book."

"BIPOC Alley, Chandler? You've become a caricature of a woke, delusional elite."

"In my research, I discovered that particular part of town was referred to as 'N-word Alley.' The n-word has no place in contemporary literature."

"If it was called N-word Alley," she says—but she doesn't say "N-word"—"then aren't you doing a disservice to the past trials of Black people by essentially scrubbing it from history?"

"First of all, I'd appreciate if you didn't use that word. Second of all, I'm *not* scrubbing it from history. Would that I could, but alas, even I am without such power. I'm just doing my part by not adding to it. Besides, the characters are still, like, hella racist in their attitudes and behavior, so I'm *acknowledging* those past struggles without *perpetuating* them."

Huffing, she says, "And I suppose you're going to make the same argument about the 'Person with Disabilities'?"

"People in the Old West referred to them as 'idiots' and 'imbeciles.' I'm not about to do that. If it comes down to being historically accurate or being a decent human being, I choose the latter."

"Okay, but I'm not sure how much of a difference the terminology makes when you're still depicting them as drooling beasts who lather themselves in shit."

"Terminology makes all the difference in the world. The depiction is strictly for scene-setting and aesthetic purposes. The *language* is what's most important when it comes to checking one's privilege."

"Jesus Christ," she says. "You're the worst kind of white person."

"Why? Because I care deeply enough about these things to give them this much consideration?"

"The only thing you care very deeply about is yourself."

"I'm not going to pretend that didn't sting."

"Good. You're not so great at pretending. You think you are, but you're not."

"I'm not pretending anything. I don't have any reason to."

"You know, you write about such awful, awful people, but really I think you're worse than any of them. At least they *feel* things. At least they aren't so *cold*."

"I . . . think my characters are usually pretty cold."

"Not like you are, darling. Not like you."

CHAPTER 8

BARTON LUMBERED FROM the cot over to the piled lump of his clothes and fished his flask out of his jacket while Caroline wiped herself off with a rag. Barton pulled from the flask, swaying on his heels, shivering. He stared at Caroline. "I could take you away from here," he said.

Caroline snorted and tossed away the rag. "Big talk, Sheriff."

"I'm serious. Away from all this. From this life. This place." He waved his arms around at the dingy room. "There's more to the world than this."

"What d'you know of the world?"

"Enough to know there's more to it than getting fucked by strangers in this shithole of a room."

"They ain't all strangers. You ain't a stranger."

Barton sat down on the edge of the bed, took another sip of whiskey. He scowled. "You can't like doing this."

"What? You patronizing me and my line of work? You're right, I don't."

"That's not what I'm doin'. I just want to make things better for you."

Caroline sat up and plucked the flask from

Barton's hand. She took a swig and started to hand it back, then thought better of it and it took another, longer swig. When she looked at him, her eyes were bright and gleaming. "That ain't what you want. You think that's what you want, but it ain't. You want someone to save you. You're startin' to realize you're in too deep and you can't keep on playin' sheriff with all them demons you got inside you."

"That's not true."

"Sure it is. You don't want to run away with me. You think you do, but it's only because . . . what? Because I look a little bit like whatever girl fucked you all up?"

Barton shook his head. "You don't look anythin' like her."

"Well, whatever it is don't matter. You ain't cut out for this, Sheriff. You come in here, holes in your arms and nose bleedin', sniffin' 'round my pussy like a lost puppy. I can't save you, James. No one can, but least of all me."

"I'm not lookin' to be saved," said Barton. His voice was hollow, weak. "I'm lookin' to save you."

"I don't *need* savin'. I don't know why you can't seem to understand that. I'm fine where I am, doin' what I'm doin'. I got more money'n I can spend. More love'n a girl could dream of. The men go home to their wives and kiss 'em goodnight, but I'm the one they love." She got up and went to the cracked mirror on her bureau, tossing her hair back and staring with avid admiration at her reflection. "That's the thing, James. You think your love for me makes you special, but it don't. It just makes you like all the rest."

HUMAN-SHAPED FIENDS

Barton had only been sheriff for a few months when he first saw Caroline. He had yet to form an acquaintanceship with Dr. Druse, and he'd never been inside an opium den. The hotel only had to send up a new bottle of gin every two or three days. The youth was still visible in his face—he was not quite thirty—and he didn't look sick. People still respected him. His dead wife remained nothing more than a memory.

Caroline came out the batwing doors with an elegant flourish as he was approaching the saloon. Barton stopped, watching her. No one else was outside, and it was dark, so she hadn't noticed his presence a few yards away. She lit a cigarette, brushing a strand of blonde hair from her face. Her eyes lifted to the black sky and searched for something there. Barton stood rigidly in place as he studied her, as if sudden movement might startle her away like a frightened animal. He didn't stir until her eyes fell upon him and a smile alighted her face. It was an artificial smile, purely manufactured, but it bore a warm radiance that could have almost passed as genuine.

"You gonna stand there gawkin' all night long?" Caroline said to him, blowing smoke out the corner of her mouth and tapping a column of ash onto the ground with a delicate finger.

Barton moved into the light and took off his hat. "I'm sorry, miss," he said. "I was just . . . I was thinkin' to myself you must not be from around here."

"That right?" Her eyebrow twitched upward slightly. "What gave me away?"

Clenching the brim of his hat in his hands, Barton said, "Well, ma'am, you're the most beautiful girl I ever saw, so I'd remember you if I'd seen you before."

Caroline laughed, and the harsh, rusty callousness of the sound did not match the quaint arrangement of her soft features and slight stature. It was the laugh of a large, hard-drinking old hag, not a pretty little vixen no older than nineteen. "I'm a whore, mister," she said. "In case you couldn't tell on account of how I'm dressed. You don't need to use cheap lines like that to get me in the sack." She pointed with her cigarette at the star-shaped badge on Barton's breast pocket. "And don't think that shiny tin on your shirt will get you any discounts, neither." Her hand moved to her crotch, squeezed. "You gotta pay premium price for premium pussy, lawman or not."

Barton flinched. His eyes dropped to the ground. "I wasn't suggestin' anythin' of the kind, miss," he said. "I'm not . . . I don't partake in the, ah, in the women here. I just come here for a nightcap now and then. And I saw you, and I thought—" his gaze dropped even lower, and he nudged the dirt with the toe of his boot "—Well, hell, I don't know what I thought. You're just awful pretty, is all, and I guess I thought I'd tell you as much."

The shrewd cynicism softened from Caroline's face. She dropped the stub of her cigarette and stamped it out with her stiletto-heeled boot. "Gee, I reckon that *is* kinda nice," she said, her voice lighter, the condescension gone. She curtsied, her tiny skirt rising near to her hips. "I'm Caroline."

Before Barton could answer, a tall, thin man emerged from the saloon. He wore a luxurious black suit which contrasted sharply with his alabaster skin and glistening white boots. His fingers were abnormally long, his eyes onyx. A top hat sat askance on his head, which he tipped casually at Barton and Caroline before offering them a brief, too wide grin that shone of dark things. "Evening, kiddos," he said, and then strode away into the night, whistling a peculiar tune.

Barton looked after him, frowning. "Who was that?" he asked Caroline.

"He's the new piano man," Caroline said with a small shudder. "Gives me the willies, but he plays like the devil himself."

"I don't much like the looks of him." He turned back to Caroline. "I apologize, where were we?"

"You was about to tell your name, I reckon."

"James Barton," said the sheriff, bowing a little.

"You look mighty young to be a sheriff, you know."

"I've been told that a time or two."

"Well, Sheriff, how's about you come on in and buy a girl a drink? Just try not to go fallin' in love with me. It'll be bad for your health."

CHAPTER 9

THINGS WERE GOOD during the first days at the cave. There was plenty of water from the nearby well, and they were able to make the food salvaged from the saloon last them for a good while. In those early days, they seldom quarreled, and even when Felipe and Innocencia sneaked off at night to make love in the desert beneath the stars, Ylario remained silent. In the daytime, quiet moments of something unspoken transpired between Ylario and Innocencia, but in the night they did not matter. In the night there was nothing to say, with words or otherwise.

But then the food started running scarce and the nights grew colder. The fires they sparked on the cave floor didn't start so easily. They were forced to eat the horses, but this only fed them for a few days before the meat spoiled. On the nights when Felipe and Innocencia would sneak out—though these became fewer and farther between—Ylario would lie in his thin blankets, twisting his hands and gritting his teeth.

Toward the end of the third week, when they were sufficiently filthy and demoralized and emaciated,

HUMAN-SHAPED FIENDS

Martín spotted a small caravan of traders some ways off to the east while he was fetching water. He rushed back to the cave and he and the others armed themselves and fell upon the travelers, killing all but one of them, who managed to escape westward on his horse, shot and bleeding. They took what they could carry back to the cave, their supplies replenished but their spirits no higher.

"The one who got away," said Martín that night as they sat around the low fire, "he saw our cave. He could lead others back to us."

"He will not make it far," said Felipe, slowly chewing a rice cake with a hard grimace on his face.

"You do not know that," said Martín, narrowing his eyes. "I did not see where he was shot."

"It does not matter where he was shot. It matters only he was shot."

"We should move," said Martín, growing bolder. "We do not know if we will be safe here."

"We are safe here for as long as I say we are."

Ylario shifted and his eyes met Innocencia's. She returned his gaze with equated unease and then quickly looked away.

"Who made you our leader?" Martín asked, acid in his voice.

The smile Felipe gave him was wan, but full of coldness and cruelty. "I have always been your leader," he said.

Back in Los Angeles, each day that passed without news of the Alvitre gang brought more unrest. The townsfolk demanded justice. The ghosts of the men they'd slain seemed to haunt every saloon, every street corner. People glared hatefully at Barton when he passed, sometimes spitting at his feet. "Where are they?" they asked him, reproachful and vehement. "What are you doing about it?"

It did not help that the paper had taken to running vicious cartoons with "the Pretty Boy Sheriff" at their center, depicting him as a wasted dandy with women's makeup, a bottle in one hand and a syringe in the other. Barton had gone to Farrington's house late one night, drunk and high on cocaine, demanding a stop to the cartoons. Farrington had shaken his head at the sheriff, smiling sadly at him before limping back inside on his crutches and closing his door. The next day's cartoon was the cruelest yet.

Barton had spoken with Conrad after his talk with the mayor and told him they needed to halt all law enforcement on BIPOC Alley. Conrad protested in vain; Barton remained obstinate. Frequent reports of crime and unrest among the Black and Indigenous People of Color reached Barton's office regularly, but he ignored them. It wasn't long before the paper ran a cartoon depicting Barton being led in chains by a hulking Black or Indigenous Person of Color.

About a week and a half after Barton called off police activity on BIPOC Alley, he and Conrad stood in the cold gray dawn outside Chiffon, an upscale restaurant at the center of town, looking at the dozens of beheaded chickens scattered around the patio in a mess of feathers and gore. Scrawled on the front of the building in blood were the words, "WE ARE

HUMAN-SHAPED FIENDS

COMING HERE NEXT TO TAKE YOUR WHITE MONEY AND RAPE YOUR JEW WIVES."

Conrad spat. "Owner said he saw a Black or Indigenous Person of Color scurry off with a bucket and a wheelbarrow just before sunup," he said.

"No doubt," Barton said, and spat. He lit a cigarette. "Get this shit cleaned up. Start with the message. Try to keep it out of the papers."

"We have to do something," said Conrad. "People have already seen it. They know the Black and Indigenous People of Color are getting bold. They want justice."

"Who wants justice? The people, or the Black and Indigenous People of Color?"

Conrad thought about it.

"Both, I reckon. But they have different ideas of justice."

"Well, neither of them is gettin' it."

Conrad lit his own cigarette, chewing it thoughtfully as he dragged from it. "You ever think maybe the Black and Indigenous People of Color are, well, justified, in a way? We white folks don't treat 'em none too good. The way we make them live, and all. Like animals, one might say. Maybe all the crime is, y'know, a retaliation." He looked south. "Maybe it's deserved."

"No." Barton spat again. "It's not justified, and it's not deserved. They are animals."

Ylario sat on a rock some distance from the cave while the others slept, gazing out at the flat night. His face was pensive, unmoving. He held in his lap a leather-bound notebook, into which he'd occasionally write something with a short stub of a pencil. When he wasn't writing, he would roll the pencil between his fingers like a coin.

The quiet air shifted. A twig snapped. Ylario reached to his belt for his gun, but it was back at the cave. A curse rose to his lips before dying upon his tongue when he saw it was only Innocencia, shimmering before him like a dream, her long white dress shifting about her slender body in the light breeze.

"It is difficult to sleep upon the hard ground," she said, advancing to the rock and sitting near its base, looking up at Ylario. "I miss my bed. My pillow. My sheets."

Ylario's eyes wandered over the sleek black tresses of her hair, shining like polished gunmetal in the light of the stars. He lowered his pencil to the paper and etched out a line of words, writing with slow, careful deliberation.

"What are you writing?" Innocencia asked.

Ylario's eyes drifted from the paper and met Innocencia's. A current came to life in the air around them, low and humming. "It is nothing important," he said, shifting his gaze back over the wildlands stretched out around them. After a moment of twisting, amorphous silence, he added, "My brother would laugh."

"I am not your brother."

Ylario looked at her, something like pain pulling at the contours of his face. "No," he said. "You are not." He looked back down at the paper. "It is a poem," he said, sheepish and ashamed. "It is a poem in English." The pencil began to pass over and beneath his gently dancing fingers. "I like English. It has beauty." He shook his head, chewing his lower lip. "Felipe would shoot me if he knew."

"I will not tell." Innocencia looked in the direction of the cave. "Felipe is limited by hate. It is justified, and I understand it, but it restricts him. There are things he will never know because he knows too much hate."

Ylario opened his mouth, closed it, his forehead crinkling as he looked at the pencil twirling through his fingers, as if puzzled by its movements. "Do you think . . . " he began slowly, his words protracted and measured. "Do you think he is right in what he has done? In what we have done?" He looked imploringly at Innocencia. "Or do you think . . . he has led us astray?"

Innocencia stared down at her lap. "He does what he knows to be right in his heart," she said quietly. "And we have chosen to follow him. I do not know what is right. I have not known for a long time. Perhaps only God knows, and we will only know when He judges us."

Grimacing, Ylario said, "Felipe says there is no God. He says he is God."

"Felipe says many things. I do not think even he knows all the things he says."

"When he says he loves you . . . is that a thing you think he knows when he says it?"

Innocencia brushed a lock of hair behind her ear and looked once more back at the cave. "That is a thing he does not say," she said.

CHAPTER 10

THE SCARLET MACAW was crowded and Barton was wincing against the noise as he nursed his third whiskey, absently dabbing a persistent trickle of blood sliding from beneath his rolled-up sleeve. It was late. The spooky piano man was playing something jubilant that had people on their feet and dancing.

"You all right, Sheriff?" the bartender asked, topping off Barton's glass and eyeing him with concern. "You're lookin' a bit pale."

"And *thin*," said a whore a few stools down, raising her voice over the din reverberating through the saloon. "Caroline told me you was losin' weight, but *hell*, you look right *awful*."

"Fine, thank you," said Barton, forcing a ghastly smile. "No need to worry. Just some long nights, is all."

"No rest for the wicked," said the whore, grinning a little cruelly.

"No," said Barton, looking into the amber depths of his drink. "They do not rest."

"Speakin' of which," the whore went on, "when you gonna catch those rotten Californios that've been raisin' all kinds of hell? The ones that killed that cattle farmer and shot up that saloon?"

"Workin' on it," Barton said.

An old man on the other side of Barton raised his head and said, "Them kids ain't the only ones y'all need to be after." He threw back the remaining dregs of his ale and squinted at Barton. "All kinds of crazy stuff goin' on down on BIPOC Alley. Those Black and Indigenous People of Color need whipped into shape. You let 'em keep wreakin' havoc the way they do, and there'll be nothin' left of this town by the end of the decade."

"Noted."

The old man started to say something else, but he was interrupted when the batwing doors crashed open with such ferocity that one of them came loose from its hinges and hung swaying from a sole remaining bolt on the doorjamb. The piano man ceased his playing and everyone grew quiet and still, looking in the direction of the entrance. A tall goliath of a man entered, walking like he had something to prove, though he favored one leg and the other dragged just so. He had a long leather duster that swept along the floor behind his shining boots, and a white Panama hat cocked slightly sideways on his large head. Around his neck he wore a string of human ears—dozens of them, ancient and dried and blackened from heat and rot.

The man surveyed the saloon. His hard expression softened, and he raised his gloved hands, palms facing out. "Sorry 'bout the doors. Guess these boots is heavier'n I thought." He spat and reached into his duster, pulling out a scrap of newspaper containing the "HUMAN-SHAPED FIENDS" article. He held it up and said, "Heard y'all got a problem with some bloodthirsty Mexicans."

Barton swallowed the rest of his whiskey and pulled himself to his feet, holding onto the edge of the counter to steady himself. "They're not Mexicans. Not full-on, anyhow. Not all of them."

The man chuckled. It was a low sound, deep and hateful. "Ain't nobody full Mexican," he said. "They's all mutts."

"Two of them are half Indian," said Barton.

Whistling through his teeth, the man said, "Even better." He fingered the ears around his neck. "Ain't no man better at killin' Indians than me."

"I've got it under control," said Barton.

The man raised a bushy eyebrow. "That so? Ain't what I been hearin'." He walked toward Barton, stopping inches from him. The brim of the man's hat jabbed into Barton's forehead. "*I* been hearin' that Pretty Boy Sheriff is too busy getting' drunk and smokin' devil flower with the Orientals to do shit about nothin'."

Barton said nothing.

"Thought as much. That's why I'm takin' charge of this here operation. It's already been cleared with your mayor. Go'n and ask him." He grinned, flashing pale yellow teeth. "Tell him David Brown sent ye." Looking Barton up and down, his eyes lingering on the empty holster on his hip, Brown said, "You look a bit put off, Sheriff. You fixin' to fight?"

Barton slowly shook his head. "No," he said. "I'm not fixin' to do any such thing."

"Happy t'hear it," Brown barked, his grin

widening. He fished in his pocket and took out a handful of gold Mexican coins, tossing them on the counter with a flourish. They rolled and bounced across the sticky wood. The bartender snatched them up. "I want your finest whore," Brown said to the bartender. "Bring 'em all out and line 'em up so I can have a look-see."

"Some of them are with customers," said the bartender.

"Not no more they ain't. That there's a lot of money I just handed ye. More'n any snatch in this place is worth, I reckon. Round 'em on up now. I don't care if you gotta pull a man's cock out their goddamn cunts. I want to see 'em all."

Visibly uneasy, the bartender nodded. He jammed the coins in his pockets, where his hand remained even as he scurried upstairs.

The other patrons in the bar were still watching Brown, nobody moving. The piano player wore a freakish, sinister grin of delight, his long fingers tapping excitedly on his knees. The whore who'd been sitting near Barton stood and pushed past the sheriff, coming to stand before Brown. She pulled on her dress, baring her breasts. "You don't need to see none of them other filthy wenches in this joint," she said. "Come on with me. I'll give you what you need."

Brown looked into her face, his eyes never dropping to her exposed chest. He spat. "Your skin," he said. "The color in it. Where's it come from? You got some Mexican in ye?"

The whore pursed her lips. "A bit of Black or Indigenous Person of Color," she said. "But I—"

"Get the fuck away from me, woman." He shoved

her. She muttered under her breath and went back to her barstool.

The bartender came back down the stairs with the remaining whores. A fat man followed, buttoning his trousers and shouting a stream of enraged expletives. A single glance from Brown silenced him. The bartender arranged the whores in a line and gestured at Brown, who approached them with his big hands clasped behind his back. Caroline exchanged a look with Barton. Barton swallowed.

"Not terrible," said Brown, pacing along the line of women, inspecting them like horses. He turned their heads, examined their mouths, made them show him their legs and breasts. He stopped in front of Caroline, appraising her longer than he had the others. With a resolute nod, he said, "This one. This is the one." He grabbed her by the wrist.

"You don't want her," Barton blurted.

Brown turned, releasing Caroline's wrist. He advanced a few paces toward Barton, his lips twitching. "No? Why's that, Sheriff?"

"She's . . . she's got the clap."

"Don't none of my whores got no such thing," said the bartender.

Brown stroked his stubbled chin. "The clap, you say? Well, let's have us a gander." He turned on his heel and said to Caroline, "Lift that dress on up, honey pie. If ye got a stricken cunt, I'll want to know about it."

Her eyes locked with Barton's, Caroline did as she was told. Brown dropped to one knee and brought his face close to Caroline's groin. He inhaled deeply. With two gloved fingers, he spread her vaginal lips and eyed them closely. When he was apparently satisfied, he stood and turned back to Barton. "Well, Sheriff." He sighed, shaking his head. "That there's among the prettiest pussies I done ever laid eyes on. Smells all right, too, which is more'n a fellow can ask when it comes to whores. Certainly don't look or smell clappy." He looked across the faces of the onlooking patrons. When his eyes landed back on Barton, they were cold and hard. "So I have to ask myself, why'd you go'n lie about somethin' like that?" He stroked his chin again, and then raised a finger as though struck by sudden enlightenment. "Ah, you fancy her, do ye?"

Barton spat, said nothing.

Nodding, Brown said, "Aye, that's it. Didn't your mama ever tell ye not to take to whores? Nothin' good comes of it, believe me. You don't need that kinda sorrow in your life, Sheriff."

"Just leave her alone is all I ask," said Barton. "Take your pick of the others."

Brown stepped closer to Barton, his dark eyes boring into him. With a cruel smile, he reached out and patted the sheriff's cheek. "Don't you worry, pretty boy. I'll take mighty good care of her."

"If you hurt her, I'll kill you."

Brown laughed and squeezed Barton's shoulder. "Oh, Sheriff. You ain't gonna do nothin' to nobody." He returned to Caroline and re-clasped her wrist, pulling her toward the stairs. His limp became more pronounced as he ascended them. His face became a taut grimace. From the top of the stairs, he looked down at the silent patrons and shouted merrily, "Don't be standin' 'round idly on my account. Get back to drinkin' and dancin', ye degenerates." No one moved until the piano player started up again, and then all was as it had been before Brown's arrival. All save for Barton, who stood sweating and trembling, pale-faced and bleary-eyed.

Eyeing him bemusedly, the whore of mixed race gave a little shake of her head and said, "Oh, come off it, Sheriff. Ain't no big deal. It's what she does. You think she just sits around waitin' for yeh?"

Wordlessly, Barton put a few crumpled dollars on the counter and staggered out of the saloon, glancing contemptuously at the broken batwing doors as he passed through them.

Upstairs, Brown shoved Caroline into one of the bedrooms and slammed the door behind him. He checked for a lock, saw there was none, and then commanded her to undress. She did so without speaking, and Brown watched her appreciatively. When she stood naked before him, Brown spat and said, "I'm goin' to hurt you some."

"I reckoned you might."

"You'll be paid handsomely."

"I should hope so."

"Get on that there bed."

Caroline did, and Brown began to undress. His body was a network of pitted scars and old wounds never fully healed. He took hold of his penis and said, "Is your pretty boy sheriff anywhere near as big as this?"

"Don't you worry none about him."

"I ain't worried," said Brown. He procured his cigarettes and a matchbook from his discarded duster and lit one. After taking a single drag, he flicked it at Caroline. It landed on her stomach, scalding her. She squealed and brushed it away. "Hold still," said Brown, and began lighting matches and tossing them at her. She did her best to remain still as he'd asked, but she could only do so for a few seconds before swatting the burning match from her reddened skin. Black mascara tears trailed down her face.

"Try not to cry so much," said Brown. He drew closer to the bed, looming over her. The shadow of his erection was long and dark and obscene. "It won't make nothin' no easier." He struck her face with his closed fist. Her head jerked to the side, spraying blood onto the wall. Teeth clicked onto the floor. He hit her again and her lower lip ripped open. "Ye can thank your sheriff for this," he said. "I mightn't of hurt ye quite so bad if I hadn't known he fancied ye." He lit another cigarette and held her right eye open. "Try not to scream," he said. "Ain't nobody comin'." He held the burning end of the cigarette to her twitching eyeball. It hissed and began to bubble. Milky fluid leaked down her cheek as she shrieked.

Flicking away the extinguished cigarette, Brown limped briskly to where his belt lay on the floor and unsheathed a long knife. Returning to the bed, he held the knife to Caroline's throat and said, "Open your mouth. If I feel ye start to bite, I'll cut your throat." Weeping and moaning raggedly, Caroline opened her mouth, and Brown pushed his twitching cock inside. With his free hand he took a handful of her hair and violently worked her head back and forth. She made no attempt to bite, though she did gag and cough, and foamy strings of green bile dribbled from her mouth.

After a few minutes, Brown extracted his cock from Caroline's mouth and flipped her over.

Straddling her from behind, he tried for several awkward and clumsy moments to insert himself into her anus, to no avail. He drew himself up on his knees, pondering her buttocks with a thoughtful expression. He then took his knife and pushed its tip into her asshole before withdrawing it with a quick upward flick, creating a bleeding incision. She screamed again, a scream that grew in volume and intensity when he forced his penis into the bloody hole, this time with much less effort. He thrust into her for a long time, so long that her screams fell away into muted whispers and her body pitched back and forth with weary resignation. When he was finally done, he pulled out and flipped her back over and stuffed his cock back into her mouth, where he ejaculated great quantities of semen that overflowed from between her lips and came spilling down her chin like hot buttercream. He remained there for a while, his cock growing soft and flaccid against her tongue, and then he stood up and got dressed. He took a pouch of gold coins from the pocket of his duster and threw it at her face. It struck her forehead and flattened her against the mattress, where she lay unmoving. Her breath was shallow.

"I'll send for a doctor," Brown said, and walked out.

INTERLUDE 5
BRANDING

THERE'S A GIRL from Monterey in my bed, reading the typewritten pages with a scowl on her face. I sit in my chair, watching her with steepled fingers and occasionally taking hits off a cigarette smoldering in a heart-shaped ashtray beside me. The bedroom stinks. It's that rank, musty odor of sex I've never grown to like, heavy and acrid. I want her to leave so I can empty half a can of Febreze over the tangled, dampened sheets.

When the girl sets the pages down and regards me with a look of horrified disgust, there's nothing for me to do but shrug. I take the cigarette out of the ashtray and suck one final drag from it before crushing it out.

"It's appalling," the girl says. "I don't know why you have to write something like that. What does it *add*? What's the *purpose* of it?"

Sighing, I light another cigarette. "It adds . . . nothing," I say. "There is no purpose."

"Then . . . why put it in? Why write this . . . this endless description of . . . *dreck*?"

I look out the window at the night, at the lights spilling down over the hills and the flat, black, starless sky. "I have to put it in," I say. I hate the weariness in my voice. "I've put myself in a corner. With my other books, there was always a reason for the violence, for the filth. There was Some Great Meaning, always. I was always *saying something*." I drag heavily from the cigarette and let my head tilt back, releasing a rush of smoke into the air above me. "With this, I'm just . . . checking boxes. This is what's expected of me now. I'm a *product*. I have to stay true to my brand."

There's amused skepticism in the way the girl looks at me. "You have to stay *true* to your *brand*? Give me a break. You're so melodramatic. You live in a world that's so far up your own ass that you're oblivious to everything but your deluded sense of self-importance."

"I do love it when you sweet-talk me," I say, wincing when I realize I've quoted one of my own characters.

HUMAN-SHAPED FIENDS

"I'm *serious*, Chandler. Like, for fuck's sake. Do you *actually* think *anyone* but *you* gives *any* thought to your fucking *brand*? No one *gives* a shit about that. People just want to read a good book. They want to escape reality for a little while and be, you know, transported somewhere else. Somewhere that doesn't take effort, that they don't have to make themselves. Something that someone made *for* them." She lifts the pages and shakes them lightly. "All you've made for people here is some sort of horrible nightmare."

"You wouldn't understand," I tell her. "I wouldn't expect you to." I gesture at the remaining pages on her lap. "Keep reading."

CHAPTER 11

BARTON WAS LYING in his hotel room, half-drunk and trying to ignore the whispers of his dead wife from beneath the bed, when a knock came at his door. He put his pillow over his face and willed the visitor to leave, but the knocking persisted. Grumbling, he drew himself up and answered it.

The mayor was leaning against the doorjamb, dressed in his evening clothes and holding a dog leash in his fist, at the end of which was one of his pet People with Disabilities. "Evening, James," said the mayor, his tone formal and somewhat solemn. "I know it's late, for which I do apologize, but I'm afraid the matter is of . . . some urgency."

Barton nodded slowly. He gestured at the Person with Disabilities. "What'd you bring that along for?"

The mayor looked at the Person with Disabilities as though he'd forgotten it was there. "Oh, you know," he said, shrugging. "I have to take them on walks now and again. Can't keep them pent up in cages all the time. I mean, Christ, James, I'm not a *monster*."

"Right," said Barton. "Um. What can I do for you?"

The mayor sucked his teeth and shifted on his feet.

"Well, ah, like I said—it's a bit urgent. And a bit unpleasant. I wanted to make sure you heard it from me before someone else got to you. Don't want you to do something you ended up regretting."

"I make a habit of not regrettin' anythin' I do."

"Yes. Of course. Well, er, that whore you fancy—"

"Caroline."

"Right, yes, Caroline. Well, it would seem that new fellow—Brown is his name, I believe the two of you met—it would seem he may have roughed her up a wee bit." The mayor coughed into his cupped hand.

Barton looked from the mayor to the Person with Disabilities, back to the mayor, and then turned and shuffled to his nightstand. He poured two fingers of gin into a sticky, unwashed tumbler and knocked it back. He turned once again to the mayor. "Roughed her up," he repeated. "Roughed her up how. How bad."

It wasn't phrased as a question, and the mayor didn't treat it like one. "You may feel inclined to . . . to *do* something about it," he went on. "In the name of honor, or vengeance—"

"How about justice?"

From the doorway, the mayor tilted his head at Barton and raised an eyebrow. "Don't be ridiculous," he said. He stroked the head of the Person with Disabilities. "Justice doesn't have anything to do with anything."

Barton sat down on the bed and looked at the floor, opening and closing his hands.

"Mr. Brown is a decorated killer of Indians," said the mayor. "He was one of John Glanton's men." He paused. "I sent for him. We need to bring the Alvitre gang to justice and I suspect he may be able to offer some . . . assistance."

"You just said justice didn't have anythin' to do with anythin'."

The mayor made a face and waved his hand. "A figure of speech. They need to be brought in, James. People have been growing restless. Or haven't you noticed?" His eyes twinkled, landing on the near-empty bottle of gin.

"I notice plenty," said Barton.

"Of course," said the mayor, drawing the second word out. "In any case, I wouldn't recommend going over there. There's nothing you can do, and some things are better left unseen. Druse is there. He'll do what he can for her."

Without conviction, Barton said, "People will demand some sort of retribution."

"For her? Nonsense. Come on, James. She's just another beaten-up whore."

Dr. Druse was exiting Caroline's room when Barton reached the top of the stairs. They stood facing each other in the hallway like opponents in a duel. Druse clutched his black leather valise in a white-knuckled hand. There was a thin layer of perspiration on his brow. He held Barton's gaze for several long moments before lowering it slowly, as if in shame, defeat. "You don't want to see her," Druse said.

"Like hell."

Druse passed his hand through his silver hair, adjusted his spectacles. "There isn't a whole hell of a lot I can do for her. I gave her something for the pain—about as much as I could without killing her. I'll be back at dawn to give her some more. She can't administer it herself." He paused. "You don't want to see her," he said again.

"I have to see her."

Druse nodded. "I figured, so I left a shot of a little something for you on her bureau. It'll put you right out." He looked long and hard at Barton. "Are you going to kill him?"

"I am. One way or another. The mayor . . . things are complicated. But I'll get him."

Nodding again, Druse said, "I'm not normally a proponent of vengeance. It's a simple man's folly. But this . . . " He looked over his shoulder at the partially ajar door to Caroline's room. "This is something different. You do whatever you feel is right. I assure you it will be less than he deserves." He cleared his throat. "She'll live, I suppose. And that's the most merciless thing of all."

"I want to see her now, Doc."

There was a sad glint from behind the doctor's glasses. "You don't," he said, "but I'm not going to stop you."

"Couldn't if you tried."

Druse nodded and made to leave. He stopped beside Barton and put his hand briefly on his arm, saying, "Try to remember, Sheriff—she's just a woman."

Barton said nothing and entered Caroline's room.

The scent of blood and sex was still dense and cloying. Nothing had been cleaned, and the gruesome evidence of Brown's assault was splattered on the wall, the sheets, the floor. Caroline lay flat on her back, not moving, a misshapen and disfigured husk. Barton stood there looking at her ruined form, his eyes bleeding silent tears. His quivering lips remained pressed in a thin, hard line.

He'd been standing there some time when Caroline opened her remaining good eye. Her bruised and bloodied lips parted in a narcotic smile, exposing the jagged shards of the few teeth she had left. "I keep thinkin'," she whispered, her voice heavy and thick, "no one will love me now. Not even you."

Barton didn't say anything. He picked up the straight-backed chair from the corner of the room and carried it over to her bed. When he sat down, he did not look at her. He only stared at his fists clenched on his narrow thighs.

"No one will love me," Caroline repeated. "That bastard took from me the only thing I got."

Again, Barton didn't contradict her.

"Do you remember when you met me?" she asked.

"I remember."

"You said I was the most beautiful girl you ever saw."

"I did."

"You still think as much, James?" The words came out choked and raw. When Barton didn't answer, she said, "I figured not. That's how I know I got nothin' no more." She coughed. A fine maroon mist hung in the air. "The doc left you somethin' in that there needle over yonder," she said. "Reckon if you gave it to me, that'd be it. No one would think nothin' of it. They wouldn't know no different."

Barton glanced at the gleaming syringe on the

bureau. He swallowed a mouthful of saliva and scratched at the crook of his arm. His eyes swung shut.

"Do this for me, James. Do this one thing for the girl you loved just a few hours ago."

Barton stood and proceeded with weighted deliberation to the bureau. He picked up the syringe, hefting it in his hand. He ran his fingers over the smooth glass chamber, the cold steel plunger. He uncapped the needle and tested its sharpness against the pad of his thumb, watching hypnotized as the blood welled up.

"Do it, James."

Barton looked at her. He set the syringe back down.

"What're you doin'? Y'ain't doin' me no favors by lettin' me go'n like this."

Barton returned to Caroline's bedside. With delicate, measured care, he lifted her mutilated head and extracted the pillow from beneath it. He stood looking solemnly at her, holding the pillow in both hands. Caroline gazed up at him, and a realization sparked in her eye. "Don't, James, not like that. I don't want it like—"

Barton pressed the pillow over her face. She struggled feebly, but not for long. He did not weep.

When it was done, he put the pillow back under head and went again to the bureau where the syringe lay waiting.

For him.

Barton awakened on the floor in the hours before dawn. The needle had broken off the syringe, presumably in his fall from the chair, and was lodged deep in his arm. He withdrew it slowly, gritting his teeth. A line of blood snaked down his forearm and began to pool in his open palm.

"Yikes, man. That looked *painful*. Took it like a champ, though. Real tough guy, you are."

Still too drugged to be startled, Barton blinked dumbly in the direction of the voice. The piano man stood leaning against the wall in the corner of the room, his arms folded over his chest and his legs crossed at the ankles. He grinned at Barton, his smile seeming to stretch all the way across his white face. "Yeah, man, a *real* tough guy. *So* tough, in fact, you smothered your poor lady-friend so you could save that noxious drug cocktail for yourself. The law and order of Los Angeles is in good hands, indeed."

Barton drew himself into a sitting position and glanced at Caroline's inert figure on the bed. He looked at it for a long time, his head swaying on his shoulders. When he looked at the piano man, his eyes were narrowed into a glare. "Don't know what you're talkin' about," he said. His voice was thick and froggy. "She died on her own. Sometime . . . in the night."

The piano man's nightmarish smile stretched wider. His eyebrows lifted. "Is *that* the truth? Just went and kicked it all on her lonesome?" He shook his head, his grin diminishing into an exaggerated frown of mock sympathy. "Tell me, Sheriff, was she kind enough to die while you slept, or did you she make you watch?"

"I was asl—"

HUMAN-SHAPED FIENDS

The piano man's face darkened, falling under a shadow of annoyed impatience. "Oh, *please*, Sheriff. For the love of our Great and Benevolent Creator, do *not* lie to me. There's no *pur*pose in it. There's no one else *here*. It's just you and me, cowboy. No one's coming. Everything is on hold." He took a square, red package of cigarettes from inside his jacket and flipped it open, pulling one out with his teeth. He lit it with a quick, nearly imperceptible snap of his eerily long fingers. "You sort of have a history of this, don't you?" he said, eyeing Barton through the smoke.

Barton went rigid. He stared at the piano man, his eyes burning hateful and confused. "I don't know what that's supposed to mean," he said.

The piano man inclined his head, fixing Barton with a look of condescending skepticism. "I told you not to lie to me, Sheriff. It's a waste of breath, anyway. No one knows lies like me."

"Who are you?"

The piano man rolled his eyes. "Shit, man, if I had just a *penny*—even *half* a penny—for every time someone asked me that ri*dic*ulous question. Look, it's not important. Trust me, I don't care what you do. I'm not all that concerned with how your story turns out. I'm just making obser*vations* at this point. And what I've ob*served* is that *you* seem to have a particular *pen*chant for killing the women you love. You might want to work on that. It's kind of a toxic trait."

Barton shut his eyes and turned his head away. "Who told you these things?" he whispered.

"No one told me jack *shit*, man. Pay at*ten*tion. I told you, this is just what I've observed. And your late wife—"

"*SHE WAS SICK IN THE HEAD*," shouted Barton, lurching to his feet, tears streaming from his red-rimmed eyes. He made his hands into fists and started toward the piano man, but the piano man stopped him with a cold, cautionary glance and a raised hand.

"Tread carefully, cowboy," the piano man said, his tone full of ominous foreboding. "No man has ever successfully struck me. You're more than welcome to *try*, but the odds are *not* in your favor." He dragged from his cigarette, the corners of his mouth hinting at a playful smirk. "I *will* agree with you, though. Your wife, she *was* sick. And after what she did, I don't know many men who *wouldn't* have done what you did. Still . . . " He gestured at Caroline's corpse. "Now you've got a *pattern*."

"She asked me to," Barton blurted. "Caroline—it was what she wanted."

The piano man nodded solemnly. "I be*lieve* she wanted to die. Poor girl had a mean streak of vanity. But I *doubt* she wanted to go in the way you took her out. Like an unwanted kitten in a sack."

"It was the kindest thing I could've done for her," Barton said, but it came out feeble and halfhearted.

"Oh, *really*? The *kind*est? You don't suppose the kindest thing might have gone into your *arm*? Listen, no judgment, really. I just think you should stop lying. To me, and to yourself. No skin off my nose, though. Do what you want."

INTERLUDE 6
LOVE AND CREATIVE
LIBERTIES

"SO, LIKE . . . WHAT?" the girl from Monterey says, looking up from the printed pages. "He killed his wife?"

I lean back against the pillows on the bed and light a cigarette. "Yeah," I say. "He killed his wife." I hit the cigarette, look at its tip burning slow and sinister, signifying something.

"Like, why?"

The smile I give her is coy, maybe a little self-satisfied. "What was in the shopping cart in *Until the Sun*? Whom did Ty shoot in *Along the Path of Torment*? I can't give you all the answers. There has to be some mystery. It's—"

"Part of your brand, right, don't make me listen to that spiel again." She rolls her eyes. "Didn't you say

Barton was a real guy? Did the *real* Barton kill his wife?"

"No." I shrug. "I took some liberties. He wasn't a drug addict, either. That I know of."

"What's with all of your tragic love stories? It's, like, a *thing* with you. Are you trying to work out your own problems with love?"

Scowling at her, I say, "I don't have *problems* with *love*. *Love* doesn't exist. Not in the way you think it does. Love is nothing more than a plot device people like me use to move characters from one scene to the next. It doesn't mean anything in real life. It's made up."

The look on her face tells me this has wounded her in some way. It also tells me I'm supposed to care, and in a way she should know better than to expect of me.

CHAPTER 12

GRADY LAY BENEATH his mother while she moved atop him, her head thrown back, lips parted, hands clasping her breasts. The creature stood watching from its crib, all its eyes wide with wonder. Its snake-like penis was erect, poking out from between the bars of the crib, straining and pulsing against its fabric sheath.

"Touch me," gasped Tabitha, taking Grady's hands and guiding them over her stomach and up to her chest. "Touch your mama like you love her."

Grady's hands rested limply on his mother's breasts as he glared at the grinning thing in the crib. His eyes kept moving from the creature to his mother. His brow was furrowed. His upper teeth were clamped on his lower lip. "I can't," he whispered, shaking his head and squeezing his eyes shut.

"What's that, baby?" said Tabitha, thrusting against him, arching her back and burrowing her hands in her long tresses of hair.

"I said I can't," Grady said again, a bit louder this time. "I can't no more."

"Can't what, baby?"

Grady opened his eyes. The creature was rubbing

its clawed hands along the shaft of its erect penis. His mother's thighs were trembling, and her nipples were hard against his palms. "I can't *DO THIS NO MORE*," he shouted, moving his hands down to Tabitha's waist and hurling her off him. She thudded onto the floor, crying out. The creature howled and began to cry. Grady leapt to his feet and took his pistol from his discarded belt. He wrapped his fist around the barrel and brought its handle crashing down onto his mother's head. A jet of blood sprayed onto Grady's face and neck. The creature cried louder. He hit her a second time. A third, a fourth, a fifth. He hit her until her skull splayed open and brains spilled in gelatinous rivers through the locks of her hair. She twitched for a minute or two and then was still.

Grady turned his attention to the creature in the crib. Its erection had withered and now its penis hung limp and deflated out the side of the crib. It reached its hands toward Grady, making grabbing motions and wailing. Every few seconds its cries would get stuck in its throat and it would go quiet, and then it would look at the mess of its mother on the floor and begin shrieking again.

"I done told you I was gonna put you down someday," said Grady, wiping blood from his eyes and cocking the pistol. "We shoulda left you out for the coyotes when you was born." The creature shook its head back and forth, sobbing and continuing to make grabbing motions at Grady. Grady raised the pistol and fired until the chamber was empty.

HUMAN-SHAPED FIENDS

Barton answered the knock at his door, drunk and disheveled. It was Druse, looking troubled. "Good evening, Sheriff," he said. He looked past Barton, into the dour dimness of the hotel room. "Who, ah, were you talking to?"

"No one," Barton answered thickly. "Wasn't talkin' to anyone."

"Odd," said the doctor. "I thought I heard . . . voices."

Barton shivered but did not respond.

"Listen," said Druse. "I do hate to bother you at this hour, especially considering your recent . . . hardship . . . but you should perhaps go down to the saloon at once."

Rubbing his temples, Barton said, "Why should I do that?"

"Well, you see, a man was brought to me sometime last week. He'd suffered a superficial gunshot wound and was nearly dead from infection and dehydration. He was in and out of consciousness for days, but I was able to nurse him back to health. I'd wanted to keep him another day or two, just to make sure he didn't regress, but tonight he insisted I take him for a drink at the saloon, and—"

Barton held up his hand. "What does this have to do with me? Who is this man?"

"An out-of-towner, no one you'd know. Name of Luther, I think he said. Not important. What's important is what he was saying to folks after he had a few drinks in him. He claims he was attacked in the desert by a gang of outlaws holed up in a cave. Four in number and matching the description of your Alvitre gang."

Barton grunted. "I'll speak to him in the mornin'," he said, starting to close the door. "It can wait."

Druse stopped the door with his hand. "No, Sheriff, it cannot. Brown was there. *Is* there. He heard it all. He's paid this Luther fellow to take him to the cave. He's assembling a posse as we speak."

Barton's hands turned to fists so tight his knuckles cracked. "Bullshit," he said. "He's got no right. This is police business."

"It is my understanding he has the mayor's blessing," Druse said, shrugging helplessly. "I just thought you'd want to know. Figured you'd want to join them."

"I don't. But I reckon I have to."

The posse was gathered outside the Scarlet Macaw when Barton arrived, chattering excitedly as they loaded their guns and tucked newly purchased whiskey bottles into their nervous horses' saddlebags. Grady Ellington was among them, looking guilty and somber. There were dots of something on his clothes that might have looked like wine to anyone who didn't know better.

"Why, Sheriff, how nice of ye to join us," said Brown with a wide smile.

"You got no right," Barton said, speaking with slow deliberation. The effort it took to keep his voice clear and unslurred was apparent. "You're interferin' with police work."

Brown put his hands on his hips and grinned wider, flashing teeth that had gone to rot. "Police work, you say?" he said loudly. The others had grown quiet. "I wasn't aware anythin' of the sort happened under your watch." Hesitant laughter broke out among the crowd.

"You're out of line," Barton said quietly.

"You's more'n welcome to join us," said Brown. "Would do ye some good. See how real men get the job done."

Barton's hands were fists again. Brown looked at them. "Gonna hit me, pretty boy? C'mon, I know ye want to. Let's give these fine fellows a show before we hit the road."

"Not here," said Barton. "Not now. Another time."

Brown started to reply, but the mayor appeared suddenly, exiting extravagantly from the saloon's batwing doors. "Ah, Sheriff," he said, smiling, coming down the porch steps. "I see you've come to see our boys off."

"Was fixin' to join 'em, actually," said Barton. "Make sure they don't hurt themselves."

The mayor waved a manicured hand. "Nonsense. They'll be fine." He clapped Brown on his broad back. "I have the utmost faith in David. I need *you* to stay *here*. No telling how long they'll be gone. We can't be without a sheriff, now, can we?"

Barton started to protest, but the mayor silenced him with an upheld finger. "I won't hear anything more about it, James. It's all under control." He regarded Barton with a stern expression that may as well have been a knife to his throat.

Barton looked at his feet. "Yes, sir," he said. To Brown, he said, "I want them alive."

"I'll do my darndest," said Brown, sneering at

Barton. "Can't promise nothin', though." Brown mounted his horse and drew his sawed-off shotgun, raising it above his head. Its ornate decorations glinted in light from the streetlamp. "*All right, men,*" he shouted to the posse. "*Who's thirsty for the blood of savages?*" The crowd cheered.

Barton watched them ride off.

'M STANDING IN the middle of the Beverly Hills Bloomingdale's, looking at a giant display that reads, "FACEMASKS: THE LATEST MUST-HAVE FASHION ACCESSORY," when someone touches my arm.

I turn. It's a woman, maybe forty-ish. Not hot, but not gross, either—this *is* Beverly Hills. She's blinking at me, a bashful smile playing around her lips, which I'm pretty sure are implants. "Excuse me, sir?" she says, her voice low and meek. She clears her throat. "Um . . . I'm so sorry, I never do this, it's just . . . well, I'm *such* a *huge* admirer of your work."

The facemask display all but forgotten, I take off my Wayfarers and put on my best PR smile. "No apology necessary, miss. Always happy to meet a fan."

The woman blushes. "Your *prose*,"

she gushes. "It's like . . . it's like the words of the *gods*."

Feigning humility, I grin and look down at my boots, shaking my head. "You're too kind, but thank you," I tell her.

She rummages in her Gucci purse, her hands trembling somewhat. Nerves? Benzos? The world may never know. "I'm reading your latest right now, and I think I may actually have it with—ah, *yes*, here we go. Would you be so kind as to sign this for me?" She withdraws a green paperback from the depths of her purse and thrusts it into my hands.

For a second, I'm thinking, *Wait, what is this, none of my books are green, is this fucking* bootlegged? But, of course, it's not. I'd know if there were bootlegged copies of my books. No, it's a copy of *Sinkhole* by John Wayne Comunale, the lettering big and purple. I stare at the book in my hands, blinking stupidly.

Now, look, John Wayne is a friend. We go way back. He even narrated the audiobook adaptation of *Until the Sun* and did so swimmingly. But . . . John Wayne and I don't look *anything* alike. Our writing style isn't even similar. Alas, there isn't much for me to do but take the pen the woman hands me and open the book to the title page and half-ass John Wayne's signature while the woman squeals.

I wish I could say I hand the book back to her and tell her to have a nice day and that's that. That's what I ought to do. But somehow, within fifteen blurry minutes we're striding across the parking garage, and then we're in the back seat of her Range Rover and my dick is in her hands and she's stroking it with amateurish eagerness, whispering, "John Wayne, you're my hero, you're my *god*," and then she's asking me why I'm crying. All I can do is look away, staring at the shadow of my reflection in the tinted window, and after I ejaculate painfully into her hand while she murmurs with delight, I pull my pants up and get out of her car, wandering around the parking garage for an hour or so, smoking cigarettes and wondering idly what any of this has to do with the Western I'm supposed to be writing.

CHAPTER 13

AFTER MOST EVERYONE had retired to their bedrolls, only Grady and David Brown remained by the low-burning fire, watching it spit and crackle, hugging blankets over their shoulders against the night's cold. Grady kept casting surreptitious glances over at Brown while Brown gazed into the flames, fingering his necklace of ears.

"If ye got somethin' to say, boy, go on and say it."

Grady flinched. Somewhere in the distance, coyotes howled and yipped. He took out his canteen and eyed Brown as he drank from it. Wiping his mouth, he said, "Is it true you was one of Glanton's men?"

"Wasn't never one of nobody's men," said Brown. "I'm my own goddamn man." He began rolling a cigarette. "But aye, I rode with John Glanton."

Grady watched the man roll his cigarette. He waited until he was done and had lighted it before saying, "I've heard things. About what y'all did down there in Mexico."

Brown didn't look at the boy. He smoked his cigarette calmly, watching the fire. The writhing yellow tongues danced in his dark eyes. "The others is mostly dead," he said. "Anythin' you done heard was from somebody who weren't there. People ain't got no business talkin' about things they ain't seen themselves."

"They say you killed innocent folks and passed their scalps off as belongin' to Apaches."

"Ain't nobody innocent, boy. All men're born bad. Women, too." He dragged mightily from his cigarette, the paper sizzling loudly. Embers drifted off in the cold breeze. "But I killed plenty of Apaches." He gestured to the necklace. "I took every one of these here ears off an Apache head."

"I thought maybe they was from Black and Indigenous People of Color. They's all black as soot."

"They wasn't always. Just turned this way after a while."

"What makes 'em do that?"

"How the hell should I know that, boy?" Brown half barked. After a moment, he added in a softer tone, one that was almost reverent, "Knew a man who could of told ye that, though. Went by the name of Holden, but everyone called him the Judge. Never found out why. I don't reckon he ever did no real judgin' of any kind. He was a great, big, beast of a man. White as a ghost and without a single hair on his whole body. But that man knew everythin' it seemed there was to know."

"What happened to him?"

"Oh, he's out there. Somewheres. Don't know where, don't want to. Had enough of that man for a lifetime. Maybe even for two."

"You don't seem like a fellow who scares too easy."

"I ain't." Brown picked tobacco leaves off his

tongue and spat. "Now quit kissin' my ass and go'n to bed, 'less you's fixin' to suck my pecker, what with your flattery and all. Which case I'll just as soon shoot you dead."

The boy's face darkened in a way that made him look years older. "Ain't fixin' to do no such thing," he said. "I was just sayin', is all."

"Ease up, boy. Not everythin's so serious. Now get. We'll be ridin' before first light, and I suspect there'll be killin' to be done."

"But Sheriff Barton said to take 'em alive."

Brown snorted. "That he did. And where is your Pretty Boy Sheriff now?" He raised his eyebrows and looked around in the dark, cupping his hand over his eyes and squinting. "Funny. Seems he ain't here." He flicked his cigarette into the fire. "If we find those savages and I say we ought to kill 'em, that's what I aim to do. So should you. Remember what they did to your daddy."

Grady's mouth tightened and he looked out across the black plains. "I remember," he said.

Innocencia found Ylario at the base of the hill, sitting against a palm tree, smoking a cigarette in the dark with his knees pulled to his chest like he was trying to curl up into himself. His face was drawn and solemn. Ylario looked up at her approach. His eyes warmed at the sight of her, then abruptly darkened when they fell to the notebook in her hand.

"I am sorry," she said quickly, looking sheepishly at the notebook. Her eyes remained lowered. Even in the dark, the bloom of color in her cheeks was apparent. "I wanted so much to read it. I did not know . . . " She trailed off.

Ylario closed his eyes and sucked on the cigarette. "No," he said. "You could not have known."

Innocencia knelt beside him, pressing the notebook to her chest. "Your words," she said. "They have such beauty."

"They are only words."

"No, you are wrong. They are so much more than words. I read them and I feel . . . I feel I am seen. No one has ever said such things about me. You look inside me while others look upon me." She put her hand on Ylario's shoulder. "You see me as no one else sees me."

Biting the inside of his cheek and angling his head away, Ylario said, "No one?"

Innocencia looked up the hill at the black mouth of the cave. She nodded sadly. "No one."

Ylario looked at her, their eyes meeting. Hers were wide and wet, full of sadness and longing and a thrumming, kinetic energy. His were timid, almost fearful. He raised his hand and placed it over hers, which still lay upon his shoulder. He held it there, very still for several long moments, before he began to gently stroke her fingers with his thumb. Neither of them had moved, but the space between them had narrowed. It was as though the universe itself had shifted, shrunk, reorganized itself with them at its center.

"Nothing can happen," said Ylario.

Innocencia bit her lip and nodded. "Nothing can happen," she echoed. But her tone did not match his, and something was already happening. The night had gone quiet and stark. All the sounds and energies of the world now resided within them, humming through their veins. The only colors were in their vibrant black hair, their flushed brown skin, their trembling red lips. Everything else was a muted gray.

An observer could not have said with certainty which of them was the first to move, to initiate contact and set something irreversible in motion. All at once they were upon each other in a frenzy, their mouths locked together, her hands in his hair and his hands around her waist. The notebook fell into the dirt, soon joined by their clothes. No words passed between them. They spoke only in hushed moans, excited gasps, kissing and caressing one another until Innocencia finally pulled away. She turned around and got down on her hands and knees. When she looked over her shoulder at Ylario, the expression on her face was both an offer and a plea.

Ylario knelt behind her, placing one hand on her hip and the other on the small of her back. She drew him into her and bit her tongue to stifle a cry.

That was how Felipe found them—coupled like beasts on the ground, sweating and grunting and groaning. He stood there for a moment, watching them, his hands hanging at his sides. Ylario and Innocencia noticed him at the same time. Many emotions passed over their faces, but they did not cease their copulation. Like dogs, they seemed inseparably interlinked with one another until the act's culmination.

Felipe went to them, unfastening his belt and getting on his knees in front of Innocencia. Looking into his brother's eyes, he pushed his trousers down around his thighs, exposing his erect penis. He gripped both sides of Innocencia's head and inserted himself into her mouth. She gagged and choked as he pushed deeper down her throat and began to piston his hips back and forth. "It is all right, Ylario," he said. "It is all right." He reached out and put his hand on Ylario's cheek, rubbing his palm over his brother's sweat-dampened beard. Innocencia rocked between them. Tears rolled down her face and fell into the dirt.

Felipe's face barely displayed any expression when he came. The corner of his mouth twitched and his nostrils flared, but that was all. Innocencia made an unpleasant noise as her throat filled with semen. She attempted to pull away, but Felipe grabbed a fistful of her hair and held her head in place. She retched, and vomit squirted out the sides of her mouth and spewed from her nostrils onto Felipe's groin.

Ylario was still pumping his cock into Innocencia, shutting his eyes against the looming image of his brother across from him. Once Felipe's testicles had been drained of their seed, he took his knife from his belt and leaned slightly forward so he could slash it in a wide arc above Innocencia. Ylario's eyes flung open. A gaping red slash appeared on his throat, spraying hot blood onto Innocencia's back with a horrible hiss. His body jerked and he collapsed onto his side, clutching his bleeding neck, his penis still erect and quivering, slickened and glistening with Innocencia's fluids.

Felipe extracted himself from Innocencia's mouth and gathered himself to his feet, mopping vomit from his groin with his handkerchief and then pulling up his pants and fastening his belt. Innocencia coughed and sputtered, wiping at her mouth and her streaming eyes. She looked about confusedly until her gaze fell upon Ylario, twitching and dying. She opened her mouth to shriek but all that came out was a hoarse whine, followed by another stream of vomit.

Lifting Ylario's notebook from the dirt and flipping through it disinterestedly, Felipe said, "You think I did not know of your covetous longing, brother?" He sneered at the pages. "And in English, no less. Pathetic." He pitched the book into the night.

Innocencia was kneeling before Ylario, weeping and pressing her hands over his, trying in vain to quell the relentless rush of blood. Felipe shoved her aside and crouched behind his brother, hoisting him up and pressing the blade of his knife to the top of his forehead. He began to cut, sawing away while Innocencia pleaded in frantic, garbled Spanish. A scarlet curtain unfurled over Ylario's face. When the blade reached the back of his skull, Felipe yanked on his hair and his scalp tore away with the sound of a shoe coming unstuck from a mire of mud. He held the scalp up like a prize. Ylario fell from his arms, shuddering in the dirt. His eyes were wide and frightened. Innocencia babbled softly to him until he was still.

"You were always going to betray me," Felipe said to Innocencia, standing and tucking his brother's scalp into his belt. "I am only surprised it took you this long."

The fire in Innocencia's eyes when she looked up at Felipe was an exploding gun. Felipe flinched, but only just so, and he quickly recovered with a smile. "Yes, there it is. I have waited so long to see such hate in you. I have tried to cultivate it. At last, I have given it life. A pity it should be directed at me. A waste." He shook his head and clucked his tongue. "You think I have taken something from you, but I have not. I have given you something valuable. Use it, nurture it. Hold it close when you go from here. And go from here you must. You cannot return with me to the cave. I expect you would not want to."

Still weeping, Innocencia started to gather up her clothes, but Felipe kicked her and said, "No. You will leave here wearing only the blood of your betrayal. When you look upon yourself, I want you only to see the reminder of why you have been forsaken. Now stand. Have some dignity and be gone from my sight."

Her legs trembling like a colt's, Innocencia rose to her feet. She glared long and hard at Felipe, and then she walked naked and shivering into the vast night.

INTERLUDE 8
THE VALLEY GIRL

OMETIMES I HOOK up with this girl from the Valley who I think is maybe the only person who understands me, can relate to me. This shouldn't be important to me, and I'm not even certain it is, but I suppose it's worth noting.

I'm reclined on her bed, lazily smoking a cigarette, staring at the battered, dogeared copy of *Along the Path of Torment* resting on her nightstand. She's been going down on me for what feels like hours, bringing me to the brink of climax and then pulling back at the last moment, prolonging it. When finally it can be delayed no longer, I push her off me and rise to my knees, stroking myself, grimacing, biting the inside of my cheek. Her big eyes are wide and doleful when I ejaculate onto her face. She smiles sadly up at me, licking some of it from her lips, and then she wipes the rest off with her crumpled comforter and we lie down beside each other.

"I had something I wanted to tell you," she says after a while, lightly tracing her fingertips up and down my arm. "I don't remember what it was. You make all the words in my head disappear, but I know they were good."

I light another cigarette, considering this. "That's a good line," I say. "I wish I'd thought of it. I might steal it."

"God, it's yours. Take it."

"Your book came today, by the way."

"So did you." She licks her lips, giggles. "You taste like regret."

"Jesus. Another good one."

"Did you start it?"

"I've damn near finished it. I kind of hate how perfect it is."

"Madness. *Madness*." She giggles again. "How's *your* book coming?"

I groan. "Late," I mutter. "It's very late. I'm so far past the deadline I don't even remember what it was to begin with."

"Deadlines are made to be tripped over," she says. She runs her hand over my chest and shudders. "Besides, you're *hot*. That's literally *all* that matters."

I want to disagree with her.

I want to tell her there are other things that matter, too.

I can't.

CHAPTER 14

MARTÍN, WHO HAD watched from the cave as Felipe committed his atrocities, had now wandered several hundred yards from the hill. He sat in the dirt, smoking a cigarette and gazing at a cactus shaped like a trident.

"Your leader's gone Cuckoo for Cocoa Puffs," came a voice from behind him. "Maybe he always was."

Martín stood abruptly, reaching for a weapon that wasn't there. He spun on his heel. A tall, thin man stood before him, dressed in black and with white skin which seemed to glow in the starlight. He wore a nightmarish grin that was too wide and had too many teeth.

"Who are you?" Martín asked in English, his voice tremulous. "And . . . what did you say about . . . cocoa?"

The stranger waved his hand. The fingers on it were too long. "Never mind. A figure of speech from another time. But please, feel free to speak to me in your native dialect. I happen to know it rather well. I happen to *a lot* of things rather well. *Every*thing, one might say." He held up one of his long fingers and winked. "Except calculus."

"What is—"

"Never mind," the stranger said again. "Listen, I'm a busy guy, and I'm only dropping by out of professional courtesy. You and I *both* know Felipe's behavior as of late is indicative of a certain . . . *madness*. He can no longer be trusted to keep you safe, to lead you. He would sell you out to save his own hide. Shit, kid, he'd *kill* you if it came to that. And trust me, kid, it *will* come to that. Sooner rather than later. Remember that when the time comes. Remember what he did to his lover. To his own *brother*."

"How do you know these things?"

"I told you, I know a lot of things. It's not important. When the white men come, you'll need to ask yourself if Felipe is worth dying for. There's no dignity in dying in a cave. There's no dignity in dying anywhere."

Martín started to speak, but the stranger was gone. He did not vanish; he was simply not there, as if he had never been there at all.

Innocencia walked in a shambling stupor for a long time. The hard and studded desert floor cut her feet to bleeding ribbons and tore scraps of flesh free from their soles. For hours, the cold of the night assailed her body and wracked her limbs with violent tremors. When the black sky gave way to a pale dawn, the cold lifted and was steadily replaced by a rapidly intensifying heat. The crusted blood on her skin moistened and mixed with her sweat and melted off her in pink rivers. Dried semen flaked from her face like dead skin. She had to squint her eyes against the burning white-yellow glare of the sun, staggering forth in half-blindness. She saw no one, did not encounter even the most basic forms of life—the sky was clear of birds, and the lizards and insects remained out of sight. It was as though she was wandering a barren, eternal hellscape, damned and forsaken.

As the sun continued its arc across the sky, Innocencia finally came upon a large Native American encampment. Narrow tents rose from the dry earth like empty, overturned ice cream cones. A peaceful, hazy smoke billowed up from somewhere in the center of the settlement. On the outskirts of the camp, not far from where Innocencia stood, a legion of horses, their legs hobbled and their hides done up in war paint, ambled about in a makeshift pen constructed from rocks and thin scraps of timber. She swayed in place, moaning and half-mad from thirst, watching the hulking, painted animals. Their braided manes shifted over their muscular necks.

A pair of women were the first to notice her. They exited from one of the nearby tents and started at the sight of her, then stood whispering to each other, gesturing at the strange, naked woman in the midst. When Innocencia didn't move, they began to approach her, much as one might advance upon a snake that may be dead, or only sleeping. She still did not move as they drew upon her, so they grew more brazen, reaching out and touching her, stroking her and poking her with their long fingers. One of them peeled back her lips and inspected her teeth and gums while the other took up handfuls of her matted hair, examining it with wide eyes. Then they both bent down and investigated her anus and vagina, pulling each orifice open and slipping their fingers inside, wriggling them around with thoughtful, curious expressions on their faces as though they might find something of interest hidden within her.

Innocencia stood and allowed all of this for what might have seemed like a long, unknowable time, until they were apparently satisfied. The two Native American women conferred with each other in their coarse dialect, and then they took Innocencia gently by her arms and led her into the camp. Other women paused their various chores to watch their arrival, rubbing their hands nervously and murmuring beneath their breath. Children ran up and poked Innocencia's thighs with sticks. There were no men in sight.

The women took her to the other side of the settlement and brought her inside the largest of the tents, where three men in headdresses and lazily painted torsos sat passing an opium pipe among one another. An assortment of scalps hung dripping on a drying rack near the back of the tent. The spears leaning by the tent's entrance were tipped with blood.

After pushing Innocencia to the ground and bowing their heads in deference to the men, the women left without word. The men stood up, slow and languorous. Innocencia rolled onto her back and gazed up at them, breathing raggedly. Her heart pulsed with haggard deliberation. The men crouched beside her and inspected her as the women had, and then one of them took a crude knife from a scabbard on his belt and started making careful, calculated cuts up and down her abdomen while the other two men held her down. She screamed, or tried to, but the noise that came from her parched throat was soft and weak. The man with the knife stopped cutting and pulled off his loincloth before positioning himself between Innocencia's legs and entering her. His face loomed over hers, huge and red and expressionless. She tried to shut her eyes but one of the other men peeled her eyelids back open.

The men all took turns with her. One or two or all of them went multiple times, and a steady trickle of semen was leaking from between her legs and collecting in a puddle on the ground. In between turns, they would cut her with the knife, drawing away long strips of skin and pressing them to their bodies, where they stuck as if glued. She finally regained her voice when they removed her lips and scooped out her eyes, and she shrieked with a terrific, piercing frenzy that did not at all faze her tormentors. She did not stop screaming until one of them cut out her tongue and ate it, his face ever stoic as he chewed with grinding determination.

When they grew tired of fucking her, one of them cut a long slice just below her navel and began withdrawing various clumps of organs from her belly, which he mashed into hard, small blobs with his powerful hands and forced them into her bleeding mouth. She died at some point during all this, but it was hours before they were through with her.

INTERLUDE 9
DAD DISAPPROVES

"IT'S DISGUSTING," my dad is telling me over the phone after reading the latest segment of *Human-Shaped Fiends*. I'm pacing around my study, smoking and sipping tonic water, casting the occasional wary glance at the leering *Dead Inside* skeleton on the wall. "It's just too much, bud. You're going to alienate your audience. Again."

"That's the thing," I say. "This is what my audience wants. It's what my *fans* want. It's what they expect."

Dad laughs. "Your fans? All, what, six of them?"

I look out the window at the sun-bleached hills. "I have more than six fans, asshole."

"What are you up to now? Ten?" He laughs again. "I crack myself up. But seriously, kid, you've got another good one here. It could be another *great* one, but you always have to make it totally ridiculous. Why is someone always getting raped? What's up with that? Why don't you try writing a book *without* rape in it?"

"It's part of my brand," I mutter. "It's what people expect from me. Christ, I can't keep having this conversation."

"Who else have you had this conversation with? One of your legions of fans?"

"No. Just some girl I'm sleeping with."

"Is she a drug addict?"

I laugh in spite of myself. "First of all, fuck you. Second of all, *no*, she's not a fucking drug addict. I don't even sleep with that many drug addicts." After a beat of silence, we both laugh. "Okay, whatever," I concede. "Look, at least thirty percent of the girls I've slept with were, in fact, *not* drug addicts."

My dad laughs some more. "Anyway," he says, "maybe tone it down a little. You won't lose anything. Nobody cares about your 'brand' but you."

"That's what the girl said."

"Sounds like a smart girl."

I think about it for a second. "Yeah, no, not really. I mean, I hear what you're saying, but . . . she thinks New Mexico is a country." I pause. "I haven't corrected her."

"Yeah, well, you always did know how to pick 'em."

I think of the Cleveland girl, wishing I could feel something. "Yeah," I say. "I guess so."

CHAPTER 15

THE SUN WAS high and red and hateful when the posse arrived at the base of the hill. The man called Luther, who had survived the Alvitre gang's ambush, was riding up front next to Brown. He looked up at the cave, which was dark and quiet and showed no signs of occupancy. "I think, ah, I think is it," he said to Brown. "That's where they are. Where they *were*, at least. I think."

Brown held up his hand, signaling the other riders to halt. With his other hand he drew a finger to his dried lips. As the riders drew near to him, he dismounted his horse and gestured for the others to do the same. They stood around him, guns drawn, waiting. Their faces were hard and tense. The sweat was frozen on their skin.

"We'll go up real quiet," Brown whispered. "If we're lucky, they's sleepin'."

"We gonna get 'em alive?" asked Grady.

"We'll get 'em any which way we—"

A gunshot rang out like a mad thunderclap, shattering the desert stillness. Birds took to the air, rising from their roosts and fluttering excitedly into the sky. The echo reverberated for what must have felt like too long. No one moved. The men looked around at each other, eyes wide, and then one of the boys from town fell to his knees. He gaped up at his companions, blinking stupidly for a moment before he collapsed onto his face in the dirt. The back of his head was a gaping red crater, smoke curling up from it like it was the landing site of some foreign space rock.

The men scattered, taking cover behind low rocks and narrow trees. More shots fired from somewhere up the hill. Another boy went down, the bottom half of his face a scarlet maw from which his tongue flapped uselessly. One of the older men took a bullet in the stomach and lay there screaming for his mother until a second bullet blew away the top right quadrant of his head.

Brown and Grady were crouched behind a large, jagged boulder. A few more shots came from the hill, kicking up dust near where some of the others were cowering, and then they stopped. "They ain't got a lot of cartridges, I don't reckon," said Brown. He spat. "Damn that Luther bastard to hell. Shoulda told us we was getting' close before we was right up on top of the sons of bitches."

"What do we do now?" asked Grady.

Brown spat again. He crawled to the edge of the boulder and took off his hat. He edged its brim out of cover and the shot came quick and accurate. Brown swore and dropped the hat, a neat hole smoking near the edge of its brim. "Bastard's a crack shot," he said. "Could pick us off easy if he's got the rounds, but we don't know he does."

"We don't know he ain't," said Grady.

"No," said Brown. "No, we don't." He swore again. The remaining members of the posse—the ones within sight—were looking to Brown for some sort of command. He gestured for them to remain where they were. "All we can do now is wait it out. They can't stay up there forever."

"Longer'n we can stay down here, I reckon," said Grady.

"We'll see."

Martín was pacing the floor of the cave, cursing under his breath. Felipe was lying prone near the cave's mouth, peering down the rifle's sights, waiting for movement. "How many rounds do you have left?" Martín asked.

"Three," said Felipe.

"How many are left out there?"

"More than three."

"Fuck. Fuck it all. I only have one shot in this useless pistol, and it is not good from this range. We are finished."

"They do not know how many shots we have. They do not know what guns we have. They do know we have the high ground."

"High ground is not enough if they decide to charge."

"They will not charge."

"But if they do—"

"They will not."

"How do you know this?"

"I know it."

Martín wrung his hands. "It is finished," he said again. "If we give up now, they will maybe spare our lives."

"They will hang us. If the choice is to die at the bottom of a rope or at the top of this cave, I choose this cave. There is dignity in dying in this cave."

Martín's muscles went rigid at those words. "There is no dignity in dying anywhere," he said distantly, echoing the stranger's words. He took a step forward, his hand opening and closing near where his pistol was holstered. "You cannot speak to me of dignity. You who killed your own blood."

"Now is not the time, Martín."

"There will be no other time." Martín took a step closer to where Felipe lay. "You, who would not even bury him, speak to me of dignity. I dug until my fingers bled to bury him while you slept. Do not speak to me of dignity."

"Another time, Martín."

"There is no other time." Martín drew his pistol.

"WHITE MEN, I AM COMING DOWN. WHITE MEN, I HAVE THE MAN YOU WANT."

Brown and Grady exchanged a glance. The others looked to Brown, scared and confused.

"WHITE MEN, DO NOT SHOOT ME. I HAVE THE MAN YOU WANT."

Brown scooted back to the edge of the rock and tried his hat trick again. When no shot came, he poked the toe of his boot out, and then his whole foot. When still there was no shot, he peeked around the rock.

HUMAN-SHAPED FIENDS

Martín was slowly descending the hill, struggling to hoist Felipe's limply unconscious body on his back. As he neared the base of the hill, the other members of the posse emerged from their hiding places, their guns pointed at the advancing boy. When he was within fifteen yards of them, Martín stumbled and collapsed. Felipe pitched to the side and landed on his back in the dirt. He stirred but did not wake. A trickle of blood ran down his face from where Martín had struck him in the temple with the butt of his pistol.

Coughing, feebly holding his gun out in front of him, Martín raised to his knees and faced the posse. "This man is Felipe Alvitre," he said. His English was heavily accented but careful and clear. "He is the man you want. He shot your men. He made me do things I did not wish to do. Take him and let me go."

For a long time, no one said anything. A low wind swept along the desert. The trees rustled. Waves of heat danced over the desert floor.

"Y'ain't in no position to be bargainin' 'bout nothin', boy," Brown said at last. "Y'all coulda stayed up there in yonder cave and had the jump on us. Coulda been all outta bullets and we'd been none the wiser." He spat. "Where ye stand now, you's a rat in a trap."

Martín blinked at him, his dark eyes soft and scared until suddenly they weren't; they narrowed and hardened and he swiveled his pistol at Felipe's unconscious form. He thumbed back the hammer. "This is the one you want," he said. "I know how bounties work. He is worth more alive to you than he is dead. I could shoot him, or you could let me go and you can take him alive."

"Where're the others?" Brown asked.

Martín bit his lip. "They are dead," he said, with hollow sorrow in his voice.

Brown spat again. "Enough talk," he said, and shot the boy in the hollow of his neck. Martín's mouth dropped open and he staggered back, tripping over his boots and landing in a sitting position. A low geyser of blood bubbled from the hole in his throat. The look in his eyes was full of confusion and wonder, and then both of those were gone and he fell to his side and there was nothing and everything was quiet.

"Hogtie the live one," said Brown. "I'll check the cave and make sure the other two ain't hidin', and then let's see if we can't make it back to town before the dead one starts to stink."

INTERLUDE 10
IT'S CHANDLER, BITCH

'M STANDING IN front of my bedroom mirror, looking into my eyes, trying to get myself hyped up to finish this goddamn book. I'm nearly there. I'm so close.

"You're the hottest, baddest writer of your generation," I tell my reflection. "No matter what, people are going to love this thing, because they love you. Now, come on, get in character."

I have a cap gun in a plastic holster on my hip. I whip it out and point it at my reflection. "This town ain't big enough for—Jesus fucking Christ, what the fuck am I doing." I toss the cap gun away and sit on the edge of my bed, blinking back tears. I need something else, something to get me in the mood. Picking up the stereo remote from my nightstand, I hit the "PLAY" button and take a deep breath, returning to my feet. I turn my back on the mirror. "Gimme More" by Britney Spears bursts from the speakers. That's more like it. I spin back around, facing my reflection, and say, "It's Chandler, bitch."

I fall into the groove quickly, mouthing the words to the song with perfect synchronization and gyrating around the bedroom, caressing my body, licking the burgeoning sweat from my arms. I unbutton my shirt, strutting toward my reflection, keeping eye contact, nearly *melting* from my own eroticism. I'm the best. I'm so hot I can't even fucking take it. I'm a god among mortals, a—

"Chandler . . . ?"

I freeze. With mounting dread, I crane my head around. The girl from Monterey is standing in my bedroom doorway, an expression somewhere between amusement and confusion on her pretty, made-up face. I feel hot blood rush to my cheeks and neck. Hastily, I pick up the stereo remote and turn the music off. "Um," I say. "I . . . this isn't . . . what it looks like."

She cocks an eyebrow, tilts her head. "I don't know what else it could be."

Pivoting, I say, "I . . . didn't know you were in town. Or that you . . . had a key."

"Well, I am, and I do. You gave me one."

"I . . . did? That . . . doesn't sound like something I'd do."

Her eyes drift to the stereo. "Britney Spears?" she says. "I'm a little surprised. I always thought you listened to stuff like Slipknot and Hawthorne Heights."

"Hey, whoa," I say, holding up my hands. "I definitely don't listen to Hawthorne Heights. Jesus Christ, what the fuck." She gives me a look that makes me terrified she doesn't believe me, so I pivot again and say, "Listen, um . . . now really isn't a good time. I'm trying to get this book wrapped up."

"I can see that."

"Look, I have a *process*, okay?"

"Right, sure." She shoulders her Prada purse. "I'll come back later."

"Cool," I say, noncommittal, distracted. My gaze has wandered back to my reflection. "You do that."

Once she's gone, I am ready. I go to my study, humming Britney Spears, and sit down to finish what I've started.

CHAPTER 16

SOMETHING WAS BREWING. It was in the air like static. Everyone knew the Alvitre boy was in the town jail, awaiting trial. They spoke of him in low murmurs, and with wary glances over shoulders, as if afraid they might conjure him or something of his ilk. Nearly everyone agreed on two things—the boy should die, and hanging was too merciful.

When night fell upon the day Felipe was carried into town, the Scarlet Macaw was packed past capacity. Men and women drank more than was customary. The piano man was playing something lurid and twangy, crooning in an otherworldly voice about a gin-soaked barroom queen in Memphis.

Grady sat at the bar, absently nursing a beer, his eyebrows knitted. When the song was over, the piano man materialized beside him. The bartender handed him a drink which he took but did not sip. He stared at Grady, his black eyes burning from the shadow cast beneath the downward-turned brim of his top hat. His lips were slightly curled in a cruel half-smile.

Grady looked up, startled by the piano man's presence. "Queer tune you was playin' just now," he said.

HUMAN-SHAPED FIENDS

The piano man's grin widened just so. "It's from another time," he said.

Grady considered this. "Didn't sound like no old song I ever heard."

"I never said it was old." The piano man's eyes glinted. He looked into his glass, swirled its contents, and set it on the bar. "You look troubled, young lad."

Sipping his beer, Grady said, "It just don't feel like justice. Hangin' just ain't mean enough for what he did to my pa. Some folks is even sayin' he *won't* hang. They's sayin' he'll get off somehow."

The piano man took a box of cigarettes from the inside pocket of his velvet jacket and lit one with a quick snap of his fingers. "They might be onto something, there, kiddo," he said. "This town is good for a lot of things, but justice isn't one of them. Never was, never will be."

Grady blinked dazedly. "Say, how'd you do that thing you did just now? With your fingers?"

The piano man ignored him. He turned around, looking over the densely huddled crowd of inebriated patrons. "No, justice is not something this town will give you. It's something you have to take."

"Take how? What you mean by that?"

The piano man waved his hand over the crowd, his bizarrely long fingers splayed. "You have a whole saloon full of angry people. Angry people who've had a mite too much to drink. People like that are easily swayed. All it takes is a little *push* in the right direction." He leveled his eyes at Grady. "They want the same thing you do. Not as *badly*, not right *now*, but I don't suspect they'd require a whole lot of convincing to join your side of the aisle, to see things from *your* perspective."

"And what's . . . my perspective?"

Gritting his teeth and rolling his eyes, the piano man said, "Christ on *toast*, the *questions* some of you kids *ask*. Listen, you want the Alvitre boy dead. The city isn't going to kill him in the way you see fit. They might not even kill him *at all*. In order for your *wish* to become a *reality*, it stands to be reasoned that *you* are going to have to *do* something *yourself*." He gestured once more at the crowd. "But not without a little help from your friends."

"How am I supposed to do that?"

"Well, I'd start with standing up, if I were you. And then I'd start talking."

Barton was nodding into a light laudanum doze when Conrad came crashing into the station, breathing heavily, his cheeks flushed. "Sheriff," he said, panting, bending at the waist and putting his hands on his knees. He looked up through sweat-dampened coils of hair. "We got a problem down on BIPOC Alley."

"Already told you," Barton said sleepily, rubbing his eyes and lighting a cigarette. "There aren't any problems on BIPOC Alley. Not anymore. Not as far as we're concerned."

"There's a mob forming. Word is they're out for white blood. That's not a problem to you?"

A low, sinister laugh rose from the shadows within the jail cell across the room. Conrad started, glaring in its direction. "Shit," he said. "Forgot he was here."

HUMAN-SHAPED FIENDS

Barton ashed his cigarette and massaged his temples. "There's nothin' to be done about the Black and Indigenous People of Color. They'll do somethin', or they won't. Simple as that. Until we get the go-ahead from the mayor, *we're* not doin'—"

He was cut off when the door banged open once more and the owner of the Scarlet Macaw came staggering in. He was bruised, bloodied, his hair disheveled. He clutched a pistol in a trembling hand. There was panic in his eyes. "Sheriff," he said. "You best come quick."

Felipe Alvitre was being held only a few short miles from the Scarlet Macaw, but after Grady had roused the patrons into action, this is not where they headed. They took instead to the streets, raiding shops, smashing storefront windows, setting fire to anything that would burn. Scuffles broke out in the road— rioters fighting over loot, proprietors defending their property, husbands battling in vain to keep their wives free from the lecherous clutches of blood-drunk rapists. The night air was soon pierced with curdled shrieks. The dry dirt grew muddy with spilt viscera.

Grady stood watching in exasperated horror. He had retrieved his father's pistol from the outlaws' cave, and he now held it limply in his hand. He was frozen for a time, as if paralyzed by the violence around him, and then he shook his head and muttered, "Ain't no matter. Don't need them, anyhow." He was turning in the direction of the jailhouse when an errant shot from a rifle struck his chest and sent him sprawling into the dirt.

Farther down the road, David Brown was leading a drunken band of petty scoundrels into the mayor's mansion, using a slain shopkeeper as a battering ram with which to bash down the front door. Once inside, they stuffed their pockets and purses with expensive trinkets and smashed that which they could not carry. When they found the caged People with Disabilities, they laughed and shot open the locks. The freed, filth-streaked beasts fled the house, hooting and howling at the night sky. The mayor emerged from his chambers, clad only in an open bathrobe and with his hair disheveled. "Brown?" he said, squinting. "What the devil is the meaning—" Brown shot him in the throat, cackling gaily.

Outside, a group of rioters was conspiring to launch a raid upon BIPOC Alley when one of them was hit in the side of the face with a shotgun round. He crumpled, his head rapidly deflating like a balloon. The others spun in the direction of the shot, only to be met with a hail of gunfire from an advancing squadron of Black and Indigenous People of Color. Other white men in the general vicinity quickly lost interest in whatever they were looting and turned their attention to the Black and Indigenous People of Color, and the riot suddenly descended into a firefight.

The streets were an outright warzone by the time Barton, Conrad, and the bartender arrived on horseback. The air was heavy with black smoke that blotted out the night sky, Bodies lay disemboweled in the dirt. Shop windows coughed out great plumes of flame. Women with torn garments and bloodied faces attempted to crawl to safety, only to be dragged off by more men. One of the mayor's escaped People with Disabilities was fellating itself with a child's severed head.

"My G—" the bartender started to say before his head disappeared in an explosion of blood and hair. Barton and Conrad leapt from their horses and scurried to cover behind an overturned carriage.

"We shouldn't have come here," said Barton. His eyes were soberer than they had been back at the jailhouse, but there was still enough of a hazy pall to suggest his inebriation. "There's nothin' we can do."

"We created this," Conrad said distantly. "This was borne from our failures."

Barton spat. "Horseshit," he said. "This is nothin' but a result of—"

"*SHERIFF BARTON.*" The voice boomed over the cacophony, cutting through it like it was the only sound in the world. "*YOU AND ME GOT BUSINESS.*"

Barton looked up and over Conrad's shoulder. Brown was limping toward him, grinning like a wolf, ignoring the stray bullets kicking up dirt around his feet. Barton rose.

Brown had a pistol in one hand and his sawed-off shotgun in the other. The shotgun he holstered, the pistol he tossed away. He clenched his fists, cracked his knuckles. "What ye say we settle this like men, eh?"

Barton, a pragmatist, reached for his holstered pistol, but not in time. Brown swung his large fist and drove it into the side of Barton's neck. Barton gasped and fell to the dirt, coughing and wheezing.

"Shoulda known the pretty boy sheriff wouldn't be man enough to fight like one," Brown said, kicking Barton in the ribs. "C'mon, kid, *get up*. Fuckin' *hit* me." He kicked him again. Barton attempted to rise, but another kick from Brown flattened him on his stomach. "Y'know," Brown went on, "I never did tell you what a right *lovely* lay that whore of yours was. Pussy like a dream, I swear. And the *tits* on that bitch—my God. Enough to make a man forget damn near everythin', I reckon." He got on his knees and punched Barton several times in the back of the head. "My, how she *wept* when I fucked her. Bled like a fuckin' pig, too. That's the thing—no matter how pretty they is, they all bleed the same."

Barton growled, forcing himself to his knees and swinging blindly, feebly. Brown laughed and delivered an uppercut into Barton's chin that sent him flailing onto his back. "You done loved her, didn't ye?" Brown taunted. He straddled Barton's torso and punched him in the teeth. Blood sprayed. "That's the problem with love, pretty boy. It makes a man weak." He punched Barton again. Shattered fragments of teeth flew into the blood-spattered dirt. "Violence is all there is. It's sex, money, power. Give yourself to violence and ye don't need nothin' else." The next punch pulverized the bones in the left side of Barton's face into crushed glass.

"Killin' me won't prove anythin'," sputtered Barton through the bubbling river of blood pouring from his lips.

"See," said Brown, "that's where you and me differ. Men like you always got somethin' to prove— to themselves, to their women, to their God. I don't got nothin' to prove. Not to no one. I just plain don't like ye." He wrapped his big hands around Barton's throat.

It takes a long time to strangle a man. Barton struggled for the first minute or two, kicking uselessly at the dirt and clawing at Brown, until slowly his kicks became little more than twitches and his arms fell limply to the ground, spread out in Christlike repose. His eyes were starting to loll in their sockets when Brown jerked atop him, and the grip around his throat relaxed, then gave way altogether. Hot blood pattered onto Barton's chest, neck, and face. Brown fell off him.

Barton lay there for a moment, coughing and gagging, rubbing at his neck, and then he pushed himself up onto his elbows. Brown lay beside him with a great, gushing cavity in the side of his head. Barton looked around. Grady Ellington stood ten paces away, holding a smoking pistol. Blood poured from a wound in his chest. As Barton drew himself slowly to his feet, Grady collapsed.

Most of the fighting had moved farther down the street by then. The sounds of gunshots had the volume turned down. The danger no longer as imminent, Barton staggered out into the open, toward where Grady lay dying in the middle of the street. He nearly tripped over Conrad's corpse, riddled with a dozen bullet holes. He stopped for a moment, looking at his fallen deputy. There was little to be said, less to be done. He shuffled on and dropped to one knee at Grady's side.

"Did I . . . get him?" Grady asked, his voice strained, hardly a whisper. "Did I get . . . that bastard?"

"You did," said Barton. His own voice was hoarse and raspy. He rubbed at his throat. "Reckon I owe you a favor. But . . . " He trailed off, watching the blood flow freely from the hole in Grady's chest. "Not much good it would do."

Grady made a sound. It might have been a laugh; it might as likely have been a death rattle. "Reckon not," he said. His eyes became sad. "I . . . did this, Sheriff. I got folks . . . all riled. I wanted . . . to go after . . . Alvitre, bring him—" He coughed blood. The leak in his chest pumped faster. "Bring him to justice. But they went . . . crazy. I couldn't . . . stop them."

"People got a way of losin' sight of their values when they catch the scent of blood in the air. Man's always just a little nudge away from chaos."

"Chaos," Grady echoed. Creases appeared in his forehead. "That's all . . . they wanted. They didn't . . . want justice. All they wanted . . . was chaos."

"They'll remember in time. When there's nothin' left to burn, they'll remember what got 'em started to begin with. They'll come for Alvitre like I always knew they would." Barton looked over his shoulder in the direction of the jailhouse. "Reckon I ought to head back there and wait for 'em."

"You should just . . . let 'em have him. It would be . . . the right thing . . . to do."

Barton spat. "I might just," he said. "Not because it's the right thing, but because I'm hurt and tired and don't have much fight in me. And there'd be too many of 'em, anyhow."

"Why . . . would you protect him? Even if . . . you could . . . why . . . would you?"

HUMAN-SHAPED FIENDS

"It's my job," said Barton, getting to his feet. "I don't know anythin' else."

He turned and walked north, leaving Grady to die and Los Angeles to burn.

EPILOGUE

BARTON STANDS BEFORE the bars, looking at the black silhouette of his prisoner in the grim darkness of the cell. "There's somethin' I have to know," he says. "Before they get here, before I decide what I'm gonna do with you—there's somethin' you're gonna have to tell me. Somethin' I just gotta know."

"I have nothing to tell you, cerdo," Felipe says. "Give me to them or do not. It does not matter to me."

Barton spits. "It's got nothin' to do with whether or not I give you to 'em. It's just something I want to know. For me."

"I owe you nothing, cerdo."

"No," Barton says with a capitulatory nod. "No, I don't reckon you do. Still, I suspect you'll tell me, all the same."

The sounds of the mob have drawn nearer. Their collective roar is a violent cacophony, an auditory manifestation of boundless rage. The floor vibrates beneath Barton's boots.

"There's not a lot in this life that makes sense to me," Barton says. "Most times I don't even try to make sense of it. I think there's somethin' dark and evil that lurks somewhere inside the earth and makes it the way it is. Lately, I've come to thinkin' whatever that somethin' is lives right here under Los Angeles." He looks at the floor. "Maybe right here under this buildin'."

"My mother and my father believed in the devil, and in God," Felipe says. "My brother did, also. I never did. There is only man and his cruelties."

"You're one to speak of cruelty."

"It is a weapon every man wields. Some men wield it better than others, and for better purposes."

Barton spits again. "Even so, I'm not talkin' about the devil, or about God. I think whatever is here in this town, whatever's behind the evils of the world—I think it's worse than both of 'em."

Felipe snickers darkly. It is a sound like the shaking of the earth. "Enough of your superstitions, cerdo. Your citizens are almost here. Ask me what you wish to ask me, and we will see if I answer."

Barton draws closer to the bars, squinting into the darkness. "All right," he says. "The folks in the tavern—I get them. You needed weapons, supplies. Same goes for the travelers you ambushed. What I can't figure is Jim Ellington. That man was just mindin' his own business, tendin' to his cattle. You didn't know him from Adam. So I ask you . . . why? Why'd you do it? Why'd you kill him?"

Felipe is silent. The sound of the mob is almost deafening now.

Barton wraps his hands around the bars. "Tell me. I have to know why."

Slowly, Felipe rises to his feet. He stands there for a moment, ensconced in shadow, and then he moves into the light, walking to the bars so his face is inches from Barton's. The space between the bars is wide enough for him to reach out and grab the sheriff, but Barton remains rooted in place. "Tell me," Barton whispers, pleading.

When Felipe speaks, his voice is like the rattling of ancient bones.

"Porque era americano."

I lean back, light a cigarette. It's not my favorite ending—that honor goes to the cruelly dissatisfying conclusion of *Along the Path of Torment*—but I think it's a pretty good one, all the same. In any case, it feels good to be done with it. I take a long drag from the cigarette, closing my eyes and holding it in, feeling the nicotine hit my brain.

I deserve a treat, so I go into the kitchen and take the fetus out of the freezer, stick it in the microwave. I peer at it through the window on the microwave door, smoking silently, only taking it out after the eyes have popped and the flesh has started to bubble. I crush out the cigarette and eat the baby over the sink, making a bit of a mess. The blood is a sickly brown color on the steel basin of the sink. Hunks of gore fall into the drain.

HUMAN-SHAPED FIENDS

When I've eaten my fill, I stuff the remnants into the trashcan and then flick on the garbage disposal, wincing at the guttural grinding noise it makes as it chops up the clogged pieces of fetus. After a few moments, I flick it back off, mop my face with a paper towel, and go into the bedroom.

The girl from Monterey is lying naked in my bed. Her eyes are open, her tan skin gone pale. A faint smell of rot wafts from her body. The sheets are stained crimson. I don't remember killing her. She may have killed herself, for all I know. I don't even remember seeing her since she walked in on my little dance routine. Whatever, it doesn't matter. All that matters is she's dead, and she's waiting for me.

I unbuckle my Versace belt, let my jeans fall to the floor. "All right," I say to the dead girl, sighing heavily. "Let's give the fans what they want."